A DARK ROOM.
A STRANGE VISITOR.
A FATAL PREDICTION.

"It's because of what's in this room," he said, lowering his voice, standing over her again, the windows at his back. "What's *inside* it." He shut his eyes briefly, and it seemed to Polly he was suddenly uneasy. When he opened his eyes again, he was staring, not at her, but at the spot on the floor near the windows where they had found Alice. He added, "What's inside for now. It could escape."

"Clark?"

He tapped the floor with the heel of his right boot. "What's beneath us feels solid. People always think that way. The fools! The ground can drop out from beneath you at any moment, and leave you falling forever. Nothing's real." He nodded toward the floor, and Polly thought she could see the stains in the wood, even though she knew they had been washed away long ago. "Drops of her blood seeped through the floor," he said. "They escaped."

"No."

"Yes. Alice's dead blood." He wiped the back of his hand across his nose and glanced down at her. "Do you know what that means?"

Books by Christopher Pike

BURY ME DEEP
CHAIN LETTER 2: THE ANCIENT EVIL
DIE SOFTLY
THE ETERNAL ENEMY
FALL INTO DARKNESS
FINAL FRIENDS #1: THE PARTY
FINAL FRIENDS #2: THE DANCE
FINAL FRIENDS #3: THE GRADUATION
GIMME A KISS
THE IMMORTAL
LAST ACT
MASTER OF MURDER
MONSTER
REMEMBER ME
ROAD TO NOWHERE
SCAVENGER HUNT
SEE YOU LATER
SPELLBOUND
WHISPER OF DEATH
THE WICKED HEART
WITCH

Available from ARCHWAY Paperbacks

Christopher Pike's

FINAL FRIENDS

Book 2: The Dance

AN ARCHWAY PAPERBACK
Published by POCKET BOOKS
New York   London   Toronto   Sydney   Tokyo   Singapore

AN ARCHWAY PAPERBACK *Original*

An Archway Paperback published by
POCKET BOOKS, a division of Simon & Schuster Inc.
1230 Avenue of the Americas, New York, NY 10020

Copyright © 1988 by Christopher Pike
Cover art copyright © 1988 Brian Kotzky

ISBN: 0-671-73679-5

First Archway Paperback printing November 1988

15   14   13   12   11

AN ARCHWAY PAPERBACK and colophon are
registered trademarks of Simon & Schuster Inc.

Printed in the U.S.A.

IL 9+

≡≡≡≡≡ Introduction

In FINAL FRIENDS Book 1, *The Party,* senior Jessica Hart returns to school a week late from summer vacation. Her old alma mater has been closed, and Jessica is now attending Tabb High. Jessica no longer has a locker of her own; she has to share one with a young man named Michael Olson. Although Jessica is charmed by Michael, she sees him more as a friend than a possible boyfriend. Michael, however, develops an immediate crush on Jessica. Michael has attended Tabb since his freshman year and is the smartest person in the school. Jessica is one of the most attractive.

Jessica's three closest friends have also been transferred to Tabb: Sara Cantrell, Polly McCoy, and Polly's younger sister, Alice. Sara is the most interesting of the three—witty and overconfident. Polly, on the other hand, is rather neurotic and suffers from poor self-esteem. But it is Alice who is Jessica's favorite: a sweet frail girl with a gift for painting. Alice has a mysterious boyfriend—Clark. Neither Jessica nor Sara knows much about Clark, only that he used to go out with Polly.

As a joke, during a morning snack break, Jessica and Polly add Sara's name to a list of students who are running for school office. There is to be an assembly in the afternoon where all the candidates have to speak.

Michael teams up with his friend Bubba during fourth period. The two boys are "Mentally Gifted

Minors'' and work on projects of their own choosing at this time. Bubba is a short, round version of James Bond. Everything goes his way, in every department—including romance. Yet Bubba is not above a little subterfuge and theft. Stealing computer codes from Tabb's administrative offices, he shows Michael how he is able to alter certain school records. To Bubba's displeasure, though, Alice walks in while Michael is using the codes Bubba has stolen. Bubba wants Alice to swear to keep the codes secret, but Alice just laughs at his paranoia.

Although Michael and Alice are close friends, Michael does not know of Alice's relationship with Jessica. Nor does Jessica know of Michael's friendship with Alice. Michael and Jessica are the two most important people in Alice's life. Alice has purposely kept them apart so that she can introduce them at "the right time." Alice has decided the time has come. She makes Michael promise to meet her at the football game that night, telling him she knows a girl he is going to fall in love with. Michael does not realize the girl Alice is talking about is Jessica.

During the afternoon assembly, Sara's name is called out, and Jessica and Polly force her to talk. Sara quickly denies that she is running for school office and also ridicules all the candidates who are running. She is elected school president by a landslide.

Another newcomer to Tabb High is Nick Grutler, an ex–gang member from a violent section of Los Angeles. Nick is tall, black, and powerful. He is also very shy. During P.E., Nick gets dragged into a heated dispute and fight with a bigoted young man named The Rock. Nick makes short work of The Rock, but only the intervention of Russ Desmond, a gifted long-distance runner, saves Nick from being expelled.

Leaving school that same afternoon, Nick meets Maria Gonzales, a quiet Hispanic girl. Maria lends him a quarter for a Coke, and they have a pleasant conversation, which leaves Nick feeling confused. Few people have ever treated Nick with anything but contempt.

Leaving school about the same time, Sara accidentally steps across Russ Desmond's path while he's in the middle of a cross-country race. The resulting collision sends Sara into the bushes. Russ stops to help her up, and Sara is immediately taken by Russ's great body and indifferent manner.

Later, Jessica and Sara convince Polly to pursue Alice's idea of having a party, where all Tabb's new and old kids can get to know one another. Polly is unsure at first because it will have to be at her house. Jessica is anxious to have the party so she can invite Tabb's handsome quarterback, Bill Skater.

Unlike the girls, who are all rich, Michael has to work full-time at a local 7-Eleven to help his divorced mother pay the bills. He is at the store when Nick stumbles in after an exhausting afternoon searching for a job. After giving him a trial task, Michael offers Nick a job. Soon, though, they are held up, but it is only a joke holdup. It is only "Kats."

Michael knows Kats mainly through Bubba. A couple of years older than Michael, Kats attended Tabb the previous year but never graduated. He works at a local gas station, aspires to be a Marine, and is pretty much a loser. During the mock holdup, Kats uses a real gun, infuriating Michael. Kats collects guns. He has a secret passion for Alice McCoy.

Michael and Nick arrive at the football game that night at halftime and are met at the gate by Alice and her boyfriend, Clark. Alice persuades Clark to wait while she dashes off in search of the girl she has told Michael about. Michael speaks to Clark for a few minutes and thinks he's very strange—almost frightening.

Alice does not find Jessica, but Michael does run

into Jessica on his own, and soon realizes the girl Alice has been speaking of is Jessica. Because he also notes Jessica's interest in Bill Skater, he does not reveal this fact to Jessica.

The most beautiful girl at Tabb is a cheerleader named Clair Hilrey. Bubba has decided she is to be his. Calling upon his considerable powers of persuasion, he talks Clair into going out with him the following Saturday. Bubba has also taken an interest in Sara, whom he sees as a kindred soul.

Also during halftime, Polly bumps into a drunk Russ trying to chop down the school's varsity tree. Because he stopped to talk to Sara that afternoon, Russ lost his race and has been kicked off the cross-country team. Thinking that Polly is Sara, Russ allows Polly to take him home. Polly keeps his ax. She also falls in love with Russ, for much the same reason she fell in love with Clark before—because he shows her a tiny bit of attention.

The following Monday at school, Michael and Nick attempt to ask Jessica and Maria out. But before Michael can ask Jessica, she asks him. Jessica has been having trouble with chemistry and is hoping Michael can tutor her. Jessica's timing is unfortunate; she never learns of Michael's intentions toward her. She continues to see him as just a friend. Nick's invitation goes smoother, however, and he sets a date with Maria for the following Saturday.

The evening of the big date comes. Jessica has been playing the matchmaker. She has talked Russ into taking Sara out, even though she has assured Sara that the date was Russ's idea. Predictably, Jessica has to call Russ when she is out with Michael to remind him that Sara is waiting for him. It seems Russ has forgotten about the whole thing.

Michael and Jessica, Nick and Maria, Bubba and Clair, and Russ and Sara run into one another at the movies. Everybody's been having a great time except Sara, who blows up when Russ asks her to pay for the movie. When she realizes that it was Jessica who talked Russ into asking her out, she runs off in shame. The big night ends with Michael taking Jessica and Sara back to Jessica's house. Michael does not kiss Jessica good-night, much to her disappointment. Jessica is still keen to get to know Bill Skater, but she has already begun to fall for Michael. Only Michael does not know.

The night of the party arrives. Half the school shows up. Polly feels she will go nuts trying to keep up with everybody. She gets into an argument with Alice. She feels Alice has lied to her and has invited Clark to the party. But Alice swears she hasn't even spoken to Clark. And it is true that Polly has not actually seen Clark in the house. The whole issue gets rather confused, but then, Polly has a reason to be confused. She accidentally sticks her wet fingers in a light socket and gets an electrical shock.

The evening abounds with interesting events: Jessica flirts with Bill, and Michael gets depressed and wants to leave; Bubba flirts with Clair, and Clair tries to get Bill into bed; Kats tries to hit on Alice, and Polly tries to hit on Russ; The Rock tries to humiliate Nick in the pool, and Nick almost drowns him; The Rock tries to get revenge on Nick, and Polly stops The Rock by throwing chlorine in his eyes.

Eventually the party comes to a close, and soon only the principal characters are left in the house. Michael, Jessica, Sara, Maria, and Nick are in the living room. Polly is outside by the swimming pool. The others are "around." Nick suddenly stands. He has to go to the bathroom. Jessica advises him to use one upstairs.

Nick walks toward the stairs and sees Bill bent over the kitchen sink, upset. Upstairs, Nick notices Kats outside on the second-story porch. Nick passes several closed doors in his search for a bathroom. In one of them he hears water running. In still another he thinks he hears someone in pain. But he enters none of the rooms until he comes to the last room at the end of the hall. The door is wide open, the light is broken. He stumbles inside, uses the bathroom, and then heads down the hall toward the stairs.

He is at the top of the stairs when the sound of a gunshot explodes through the house. Instinctively, Nick runs down the stairs, accidentally banging into Maria, who is running up the stairs.

Michael, Sara, Jessica, and Polly join Maria and Nick upstairs. Together they enter the dark bedroom at the end of the hall. They turn on a corner lamp. Kats, Bill, Bubba, Clair, and The Rock—in that order—come up behind them.

On the floor, in a pool of blood with a gun in her mouth and a hole in the back of her head, is Alice.

They bury Alice a few days later. Everyone assumes it was a suicide. But Michael knows his dear friend would never have killed herself. When Jessica does not share his point of view, he yells at her, breaking her heart and his own.

FINAL FRIENDS Book 1, *The Party,* ends with Michael vowing to find the person who murdered Alice.

CHAPTER ONE

I can't wear glasses to school," Jessica Hart said. "I'll look like a clown."

"But you can't see without them," Dr. Baron said.

"I don't care. There's nothing worth seeing at Tabb High, anyway. I won't wear them."

The eye examination was over. Beside her best friend, Sara Cantrell, Jessica was seated on a hard wooden chair in front of Dr. Baron's huge walnut desk. Jessica had been coming to Dr. Baron since she was a child. A slightly built, kindly faced man with beautiful gray eyes and neatly combed gray hair, the ophthalmologist had changed little throughout the years. Unfortunately, neither had his diagnosis. He continued to say her eyesight was failing.

"Jessie," Sara said. "Even with your old glasses on, you almost ran over that kid on the bike on the way here."

"What kid?" Jessica asked.

"I rest my case," Sara muttered.

Dr. Baron, as patient as when Jessica had been six and didn't want to peer through his examination equipment because she feared her lashes would stick to the eyepieces, folded his fine hands on top of his neatly polished desktop. "You may be pleasantly surprised, Jessie, at the number of attractive frames this office has obtained since your last exam. Glasses have recently become something of a fad. Look at the number of models wearing them on magazine covers."

Models on magazines aren't worried about being

voted homecoming queen, Jessica thought. "How about if I try the soft contacts again?" she asked. "I know last time my eyes had a bad reaction to them, but maybe they'll be OK now."

"Last time you started bawling whenever you had to put them in," Sara said.

"That's not true," Jessie said. "I didn't give myself a chance to get used to them."

"A few people," Dr. Baron said, "less than one in a hundred, have hypersensitive eyes. The slightest bit of dust or smoke makes their eyes water. You are one of those people, Jessie. You have to wear glasses, and you have to wear them all the time."

"What if I sit in the front row in every class?"

"You do that already," Sara said.

"What if I only put them on when I'm in class, and take them off afterward, at lunch and stuff?" Jessica asked.

Dr. Baron shook his head. "If you start that, you'll be taking them off and on between each class, and your eyes will have to keep readjusting, and that'll cause strain. No, you are nearsighted. You have to face it." He smiled. "Besides, you're an extremely attractive young lady. A nice pair of glasses is hardly going to affect how others see you."

Sara chuckled. "Yeah, four eyes."

"Hardy, ha," Jessica growled. Homecoming was only two weeks away, and she was beginning to have grave doubts about the "attractive," never mind the "extremely." If not for the piercing headaches that had begun to hit her every day after school—and which she knew were the result of eyestrain—she wouldn't even have stopped in for an eye exam. She would simply have waited until after homecoming. But now she was stuck. Sara would hassle her constantly to put on her glasses.

"One thing I don't understand," Jessica said. "Why

has my vision gone downhill so rapidly in the last few months? I mean, I don't have some disease that's making me blind, do I?''

"No, definitely not," Dr. Baron said. "But sometimes a stressful period can worsen an individual's sight at an accelerated rate." He raised an inquiring eyebrow. "Have you been under an unusual amount of pressure?''

The memory of Alice's death needed only the slightest nudge to flood down upon her in a smothering wave. Red lips around a black gun. Red blood dripping through beautiful yellow hair. Closed eyes, forever closed. Jessica lowered her head, rubbed her temples, feeling her pulse. It was hard to imagine a time when she would be able to forget. Alice had been with her the last time she had visited Dr. Baron's office. "I suppose," she answered softly.

The good doctor suggested she browse through the frames in the next room while he examined another patient. Jessica did so without enthusiasm, finally settling on an oversize pair of brown frames that Sara thought went well with her brown hair and eyes. Before they left, Dr. Baron reappeared, promising the glasses would be ready the following Monday. Only four days, and it used to take four weeks. Jessica thanked him for his time.

They had left Polly McCoy waiting in the car; Polly had wanted it that way. She was listless these days. Often, she would sit alone beneath a tree at school during lunch and stare at the clouds until the bell rang. She ate like a bird. She had lost twenty pounds in the last two months since she had lost her sister Alice. It was weird, she looked better than she had in years—as long as one didn't look too deeply in her faraway eyes and ponder what might be going on behind them. Jessica worried about her constantly. Yet Polly insisted she was fine.

3

"Do you need new glasses?" Polly asked, shaking herself to life in the backseat as Jessica climbed in behind the wheel and Sara opened the passenger door.

"She's blind as a bat," Sara said.

"I can see just fine," Jessica said, starting the car with the window up. It was the beginning of December, and after an unusually long, lingering summer, the sun had finally decided to cool it. Heavy gray clouds were gathering in the north above the mountains. The weatherman had said something about a storm in the desert. Flipping the heat on, Jessica put the car in reverse and glanced over her shoulder.

"Watch out for the kid on the bike," Sara said.

"What kid?" Jessica demanded, hitting the brakes and putting the car in Park. Then she realized Sara was joking. "I was going to put them on in a second," she said, snatching her old glasses from her bag.

"I seriously doubt a single potential vote is going to see you on the way home," Sara said.

"That's not why I hate wearing them," Jessica said, putting on the specs and wincing at how they seemed to make her nose stick out in the rearview mirror.

"I heard Clair Hilrey's a patient of Dr. Baron, too," Sara said.

"Really?" Jessica asked. The talk around campus had it that it was between Clair and her for homecoming queen. Jessica wondered. The results of the preliminary homecoming court vote wouldn't be announced until the next day, Friday. Wouldn't it be ironic if neither of them was even elected to the court?

It would be a disaster.

Sara nodded seriously. "He's prescribed blue-tinted contacts for her to make her eyes sparkle like the early-morning sky."

Jessica shoved her away. "Shut up!"

Sara laughed, as did Polly, although Jessica doubted Polly felt like laughing.

They hit the road. Sara wanted to go to the bank to get money from the school account. She needed cash, she said, to pay for the band that was to play at the homecoming dance. A month earlier, acting as ASB—Associated Student Body—president, Sara had cleverly talked a local car dealer into donating a car to the school in exchange for free advertising in Tabb's paper and yearbook. The car had been the grand prize in a raffle put on to raise money for Tabb's extracurricular activities. The raffle had been a big success, and Sara now had several grand to put into the homecoming celebrations.

Jessica, however, did not want to go to the bank. She was getting another headache, and besides, she had someone to see. With hardly a word, she dropped both girls off at Sara's house. Sara could always give Polly a ride home. She'd finally gotten her license back. These days Sara was always quick to help Polly out.

Things have changed.

But life goes on—Jessica knew it had to go on for her. She had mourned Alice for two months. She had gone directly home after school each day. She had spent most of her time in her room, neither listening to music nor watching TV. She had spent the time crying, and now she was sick of crying. Alice was gone. It was the most terrible of terrible things. But Jessica Hart was alive. She had to worry about her looks again, whether Bill Skater found her desirable, whether she was going to pass her next chemistry exam. She had to live. But before she could properly start on all those things, she had to heal the rift between Michael Olson and her. It was time they talked.

She had obtained his address from the phone book. She preferred seeing him at his house rather than speaking to him at school. She hardly saw him on

5

campus, anyway. He came and he went, he said hello and he said good-bye. It was her hope that he would feel more sociable on his own turf.

With the help of a map, she located his place, parking a hundred yards up the street from the small white-stucco house. The late-afternoon sun was ducking in and out of drifting clouds. She looked around: secondhand cars leaking oil on top of broken asphalt driveways; backyards with weeds instead of pools. This wasn't her kind of neighborhood, and she realized the truth of the matter with a mild feeling of self-loathing. Nice things meant too much to her.

His garage was open, but she didn't see his car. She briefly wondered if he was at work, but remembered that he always took Thursdays off. She decided to wait. After pulling on a sweater, she reached for her SAT practice test book. The real test was to be a week from Saturday. With all her studying, she had only begun to score over a thousand. Compared to the average college-bound student, this was a respectable score, but next to the typical Stanford freshman—which she hoped to be this time next year—she was at the bottom of the pile. The math sections were what was killing her. She could figure out most of the problems; she simply couldn't figure them out quickly enough.

They raise us with calculators in our hands and then take them away precisely when we need them most.

Jessica picked up a pencil and set the timer on her dashboard clock. She vowed to run through as many math tests as it took for Michael to show up.

She dozed briefly in the middle of the third round, but a couple of hours later, when Michael Olson's beat-up Toyota pulled into his garage, she was still there. However, she did nothing but watch as he climbed out of his car and stretched in the orange evening light for a moment before disappearing inside.

She remembered eight weeks earlier when he had cursed her for assuming Alice had committed suicide. And she remembered her inability to defend herself, to explain how it couldn't have been any other way.

Suddenly she was afraid to see him. Yet she did not leave. She simply sat there, staring at his house.

CHAPTER TWO

How much cash did you get?'' Polly asked as Sara returned to the car from a quick stop inside the bank.

''Three grand,'' Sara said, closing the door, setting down her bag, and reaching for the ignition. She never wore a seat belt. If she was going to be in a major accident, she was already convinced her car would explode in flames. She had that kind of luck. The last thing she wanted was to be tied in place. ''I have to pay the band, the caterer, and that circus guy who's renting us the canopy.''

Homecoming would be a lot different this year, Sara thought, and a lot better. She again complimented herself on insisting at the start of the year that the dance be postponed until basketball season. The delay had given her time to raise the money necessary to put on a wild celebration that everyone could enjoy for a nominal fee, rather than a stuffy party that only a few could afford.

The plan was to have the dance at the school immediately after the first home game, outside, on the practice basketball courts. When she had initially proposed the idea to the ASB council, they had all told her she was mad. ''We come to this goddamn school

7

every goddamn day," the beautiful, bitchy vice-president Clair Hilrey had said. "We can't stage an event as crucial as the crowning of the new queen between the peeling gym and the stinking weight room!"

Naturally, the negative reaction had only strengthened Sara's belief she was on to something. Yet the idea had its potential problems. What if it rained that night? And equally as bad, how could they create a party atmosphere when they would be surrounded by nothing but dark?

It was then Sara had thought of renting a giant tent. What a genius! With a tent the whole school could come; everybody, whether they had a date or not. And they could decorate it any way they wanted, and have a live band with the volume turned way up. Clair had loudly booed the idea, along with every other so-called hip person on the council. But the others in the room, those who figured they wouldn't be going to the dance, had nodded thoughtfully at the suggestion. That was enough for Sara. She hadn't even put it to a vote—she had simply gone about making preparations.

"You were able to get all that money on your own signature?" Polly asked.

"No, it's a joint account," Sara said. "I needed the treasurer's signature, too. Bill Skater signed a check for me this afternoon."

"Before you wrote in the amount?"

"What's your problem?" Sara snapped, before remembering she had promised herself she would be nice to Polly until Polly was fully recovered from Alice's suicide. Polly turned away at the change in tone, nervously tugging on a bit of her hair. Except for a streak of gray that had mysteriously sprung from beside her right ear, she looked—in Sara's truly unbiased opinion—downright voluptuous. That was what happened when fat girls got skinny. Why did anyone

8

pay for breast implants? Probably pigging out for a few months and then going on a fast would work just as well.

"I was only asking," Polly said defensively. "It's not safe carrying around that much cash. It's better to pay people with checks. That way you get a receipt, too."

"I realize that," Sara said patiently. "But take the band. None of them want to declare this money on their income tax. I can dangle the cash in their faces and tell them to make me an offer I can't refuse. And they'll make it."

"Isn't that against the law?"

"I don't know. Who cares? Hey, has that engineer at your parents' company finished designing the float?" Another plus, in Sara's mind, of having the homecoming dance in a tent was that simply by pulling aside a flap, a special platform could be driven in for the crowning. The old custom of having the princesses cruise onto the track surrounding the football field with their papas had struck Sara as—well, old-fashioned. She had envisioned a castle float, with a central tower that the queen would ascend after the opening of the secret envelope. She had stolen the concept from a video on MTV.

"You mean Tony?" Polly said. "Yeah, he called last week. He has it all worked out. He said he can use one of the trucks at the company to build it on."

"Great." That was one thing she wouldn't have to pay for.

"It's going to have to be towed to the tent," Polly said. "And Tony warned me that we'll need a good driver. It'll be hard to see, and the float won't be real stable."

"I'll think of someone."

"I don't want to do it," Polly said quickly.

"OK."

"I don't."

"That's fine."

Polly nodded, relaxing. "All right."

Sara gave her a hard look and sighed to herself. Who was she fooling? Polly was never going to get over Alice. None of them were. Sara hadn't even told Jessica this, but she could no longer stand to be alone. Occasionally she wondered if some sick impulse would suddenly strike her, like a demon whispering in her ear. And, like Alice, she would grab a knife, or maybe a razor blade, and cut open a vein, and bleed all that blood Alice had. . . .

But, no, she was not suicidal and never had been. She was in no hurry to leave this world. Yet she would have given a great deal to see Alice again, even for a few minutes. Two long months, and still her grief was an open wound.

Before pulling away from the bank, Sara noticed the teller had forgotten to stamp the new balance in the ASB council's checkbook. A dash back inside remedied the situation.

On the way to Polly's house, they talked about Polly's guardian aunt. The poor old lady had had a mild heart attack immediately after hearing about Alice, and had only recently returned home. A nurse watched her during the day while Polly was in school, but Polly took care of her the rest of the time: cooking her food, rubbing her back, helping her to the bathroom. Sara admired Polly's charity but didn't understand—with the bucks Polly had—why she didn't hire round-the-clock help. She'd get a lot more sleep that way.

After Sara dropped Polly off, she stopped by the market. Only this market wasn't just any market. It was six miles out of her way, below par in cleanliness, and had an employee named Russ Desmond. She had asked around campus—discreetly, of course—where he worked. This would be her fourth visit to the store. The previous three times he had either been off or working in the back.

Naturally, she saw him practically every day at school, but being ASB president, she thought it beneath her dignity to go chasing after him there.

Starting in produce, her bag in her hand, she went up and down every aisle until she came to the meat section. She didn't see him. More disappointed than she cared to admit, she was heading for the exit when she spotted him wheeling a pallet into the frozen-food section. He had on a heavy purple sweater, orange gloves, and a green wool cap that was fighting a losing battle with his bushy brown hair.

What a babe.

She didn't know why he looked so good to her. Most girls would have thought he had too many rough edges and was too sloppy to be handsome. Actually, she thought that herself; nevertheless, she always got a rush when she saw him. She liked the curve of his powerful shoulders, the insolence in his walk. Yet she didn't for a moment believe she was infatuated with him. She was too cool to be suffering from something so common.

She wanted him to notice her, to call her over. Acting like an ordinary, everyday shopper, she began to browse through the ice cream and Popsicles, drawing closer and closer to where he was working. She had approached within ten feet of him, and still he hadn't seen her. Feeling mildly disgusted, she finally spoke up.

"Hey, Russ, is that you?"

He glanced up. "Sara? What are you doing here?"

She shrugged. "Shopping. You work here?"

"Yeah."

"I didn't know that. I come in here all the time."

"Really? I've never seen you before."

"I usually don't stay long. In and out—you know how it is."

"Huh." He returned to unloading his pallet, bags of frozen carrots. "What are you looking for?"

"What?"

"What are you buying?"

"Oh—Spam."

"Aisle thirteen, lower shelf on the right. You like Spam?"

"It's all right."

"I can't stand it."

Neither could she. "I like the cans." Brilliant. She cleared her throat. "So, what's new?"

"Nothing. What's new with you?"

"Oh, just putting the homecoming dance together. You know I'm ASB president?"

"I remember you said that, yeah."

"It's in a couple of weeks." *Hint, hint, hint.* She didn't exactly have a date yet. Actually, no guy had even spoken to her in the last month. For all he cared. He finished with his carrots and went on to broccoli. She added, "I'm going."

"Huh."

"Yeah, I have to. I open the envelope that announces the new queen." She paused, swallowed. "Are you going?"

"Nah. What for?"

"To have fun. We're going to have a neat band. They're called the Keys. I heard them a few days ago. They play great dance music. Do you like to dance?"

"Sometimes, yeah. When I'm drunk enough."

She didn't know how to respond to that. Booze wasn't allowed at the dance. She stood there feeling totally helpless for the next minute, reading and rereading the label on a bag of frozen cauliflower—"Ingredients: Cauliflower"—while Russ finished with his vegetables. He began to collect his empty boxes,

12

stacking them on his pallet. "I've got to go in back," he said.

"OK."

He didn't invite her to accompany him, but she followed him anyway. Fortunately, there wasn't anybody else in the back, not beside the frozen-food freezer. Sara could hardly believe the cold rushing out of it or how Russ could work inside it. He began to restock his pallet, his breath white and foggy. He was a superb worker. He never stopped moving. He had excellent endurance. She remembered something she wanted to bring up.

"I hear you're going to be in the CIF finals," she said. It was extremely difficult to even qualify for the CIF—California Interscholastic Federation—finals.

"It's no big deal," he said, going farther into the freezer, disappearing around several tall stacks of boxes. She took a tentative step inside, feeling goose-flesh form instantly. She noted the huge ax strapped to the inside of the frost-coated door.

"Sure it is," she called, hanging the strap of her bag around a dolly handle, cupping her fingers together. She couldn't even see him.

"Lots of people qualify," he called.

"But I bet you win," she called back.

"What?"

For some reason, shouting in the dark—particularly when you were repeating yourself—had always struck Sara as one of the most ridiculous things a human being could do. "I said, you'll probably win!"

"That shows how much you know about cross-country," he said, reappearing with his arms laden with boxes.

That sounded like an insult, and here she was trying to compliment him. "I know something about it," she said. She had been closely following his performances in the papers. He had won his last ten races, improving his time with each meet.

"Sure," he said.

"I do."

"What do you know?"

"That if you break fourteen minutes, you'll win."

He snorted. "Of course I'd win if I broke fourteen minutes. But the finals are down in Newport, on the hilliest course in the city. *Fifteen* minutes will be tough." He dumped his boxes on the pallet, muttering under his breath, "I'm not going to win."

"Don't say that. If you say that, you won't win."

"Who cares?"

"What do you mean, who cares? Don't you care?"

"Nope."

She had begun to shiver. Another minute in there and her hair would turn white. But at the same time she could feel her blood warming—or was it her temper? "What are you saying?"

"That I don't care." He pulled off his gloves, rubbed his hands together. "It's just a goddamn race."

"A goddamn race? It's the city championship! If you win, they'll give you a goddamn scholarship!"

He shook his head. "I ain't going to college. I can't stand going to high school."

"I don't believe it," she said, disgusted. "Here you have this tremendous natural talent that can open all kinds of doors for you and you're just going to throw it away? What the hell's the matter with you?"

He looked at her, frowned. "Why are you always shouting at me?"

"Shouting at you? When have I shouted at you? I haven't even spoken to you in two whole months!"

"Yeah, but the last time you did, you were shouting at me."

"Well, maybe you need someone to shout at you. Get you off your ass. The reason you don't care is because you drink too much. You're seventeen years old and you're already a drunk!''

"I'm eighteen."

"You're still a drunk. I've seen you run. If you didn't down a case of beer every evening, you'd probably be in the Olympics."

He didn't like that. "Who are you to tell me what I should do? You're as screwed up as anybody."

"And what's that supposed to mean?"

He stood. "You're insecure. Every time I talk to you—it doesn't matter for how long—you tell me you're the president of the school. All right, I heard you the first time. And who cares? I don't. I don't care if you're the Virgin Mary."

Sara couldn't believe what she was hearing. Insecure? She was the most together teenager since Ann Landers and Dear Abby had gone to school. She was so far out that she had been nominated for school president when she wasn't even running— Well, that was only one example of how far out she was. There were dozens of others. "Who are you calling a virgin?" she demanded.

He laughed. Why was he laughing? She'd give him something to laugh about. She stepped forward, shoved him in the chest. "Shut up!" she shouted.

He laughed harder. "That's it. That's your problem, Sara. You don't need a date for homecoming, you need a good roll in the hay."

Sara clenched her fists, her fingernails digging into her palms. She clenched them so tightly she knew she'd be able to see the marks the next day. If she hadn't done this, she probably would have ripped his face off. Only one other time in her life had she ever felt so humiliated: the last time she had spoken to Russ, at the end of their ill-fated date. She sucked in a breath, taking a step away from him rather than toward him. "What makes you think I don't have a date?" she asked softly.

He stopped laughing, glanced at the floor, back up at her—still grinning. "That's why you came in here, isn't it? I saw you looking for me."

She smiled slowly, faintly. "I was looking for you?"

"Yeah. I think you were."

"I was looking for a can of Spam," she said flatly.

He lost his grin. "Sara, there's nothing wrong with—"

"Stop," she said, taking another step back, her hand feeling for the edge of the freezer door. "Just stand perfectly still and don't say another word."

His eyes darted to her hand, panic twisting his face. "Wait! The inside lock—"

She slammed the door in his face. On the way out, she picked up a can of Spam in aisle thirteen. She had decided to have it for dinner.

Yet she shook as she drove home. She wasn't worried Russ would freeze to death—if worse came to worst he could always chop his way out—she was worried he had been right about her.

Only much later did she realize she had left her purse in the store.

CHAPTER THREE

The sound startled Michael Olson. Standing in the middle of his garage beside his homemade telescope, he paused to pinpoint its source, then laughed out loud at his foolishness. He had made the noise himself; he had been whistling. He used to whistle all the time, but this was probably the first time since the McCoys' party. He had forgotten what it sounded like to be happy.

Am I? I can't be.

The truth of the matter was that he felt fine, not overflowing with joy, but pretty good. And with that realization came a flicker of guilt. He had promised himself at Alice's funeral that he would never let himself feel again, that he would never give pain such a clear shot at him. But that had been childish, he saw that now. He had actually seen that for a couple of weeks now, although he had not stopped to think about it. He reached out and touched his twelve-inch reflector telescope, the hard aluminum casing, the well-oiled eyepiece knob. To a certain extent, the instrument was to thank for his comeback.

For two weeks after his blowup with Jessica, he had stayed away from school. During that time, he had done nothing: he had not cried; he hadn't thought about who had killed Alice. Indeed, he had hardly thought about Alice at all, or rather, he had thought about nothing else, but without the comfort of allowing her sweet face to enter his mind. He had blocked every happy thought associated with her, picturing only her coffin, the gun, the weight of her dead body when he had accidentally kicked it in the dark bedroom. He had censored his thoughts out of shame— not just because he felt partially responsible for her death.

All his life people had told Michael what a cool guy he was. And in his immense humility—what a laugh— he had always lowered his eyes and shook his head, while at the same time thinking that he must, in fact, be quite extraordinary. He excelled in school. He worked hard. He helped his mother with the bills. He helped lots of people with their homework. He did all kinds of things for all kinds of people who weren't quite so neat as himself.

That was the crux of the matter right there. He performed these good works, but he did so mainly to reinforce his image. This did not mean he was a completely evil person—only a human being. The day of the funeral had made that all too clear, although it had taken him a while to assimilate the full meaning of his behavior. He had handled every sort of emotion since he was a child by bottling it up. But grief—crushing grief—had shattered Mr. Far-out Michael Olson. He hadn't been able to handle it at all. He had lashed out like a baby, attacking Jessica just when she was hurting the most. Yeah, he was human all right, and still in high school.

Exactly two weeks after the party, he'd had a sudden urge to drive out to the desert. The evening had been clear, the orange sand and rocks sharp and warm. When the sun had set and the stars came out, he lay on his back on top of a hill, miles from the nearest person, letting his thoughts wander the course of the Milky Way. Perhaps he had dozed. Maybe he had dreamed. He remembered lying there a long time, enjoying the first real rest he'd experienced since Alice's death. A calm, solid strength seemed to flow into him from the ground, and it was as if *something* else had touched him, something deep and powerful. He would have said it had come from above, from the stars, had it not touched so close to his heart. To this day, he couldn't say what had happened, except that for approximately two hours he had felt loved, completely loved.

By *whom* or *what* he didn't know.

Michael had never thought much about God. At a fairly early age, he had come to the conclusion that there might be one, but that it would be a sheer waste of time trying to prove it. He still held that opinion.

But now he did feel there was *something* wonderful out there in the cosmos, or inside him—either place, it didn't matter. His feeling was more intuitive than logical. Then again, it could have been a desperate invention of his overly grieved heart, but he didn't care. It gave him comfort. It allowed him to remember Alice as she had been, without feeling pain.

When he had finally returned home that night, he dreamed of the girl he had dreamed about a couple of weeks before Alice had died. He had been on the same bridge, the same blue water flowing beneath him, the identical desert in front, the forest at his back behind the girl. Again, she had not allowed him to turn to see her, again saying something about a veil. But she had leaned close to his ear, to where he had felt the brush of her hair against his cheek. It had been the touch of her hair that had awakened him. He wished it hadn't. She had been on the verge of revealing something to him, he was sure, something different.

He had started on his telescope the next day, buying the grinding kit for the mirror from a downtown shop, purchasing other accessories as he went along: the aluminum tubing, the rack-and-pinion casing for the oculars, the eyepieces themselves—constructing the stand and clock drive from scratch. This was by no means his first experience at building a telescope. He had put together a six-inch reflector in eighth grade. But doubling the size of the aperture had squared the complexity of the undertaking. Yet working on it did give him much satisfaction.

He returned to school, and the telescope became central to his MGM (Mentally Gifted Minors) project. He designed it with an unusually short focal point, making it poor for high-resolution work—such as would be required for studying the moon and the planets—but giving it a wonderfully wide field of view, ideal for examining huge star groups. He explained to his project adviser that he was looking for comets. That was only a half-truth.

He was actually searching for a *new* comet.

It was a fact that the majority of comets were discovered by amateur astronomers working with fairly modest equipment. The odds against his making such a discovery, however, even after a dozen years of careful observation in the darkest desert nights, should have been a thousand to one. It was a strange universe out there.

Then just two weeks ago, searching from the top of the hill where he had begun his comeback, he charted a faint wisp of light close to the star Sirius that had—as far as he could tell—never been charted before.

He had followed the light for several days, and "followed" was the word for it; the light was moving. It wasn't a nebula or a galaxy or globular cluster. It was definitely a comet. Perhaps it was *his* comet. He needed to complete a more detailed positional record before he could submit a formal application to a recognized observatory requesting verification of his discovery.

Unfortunately, the recent poor weather was frustrating his efforts. It had been cloudy in the desert the whole past week, and there was no way he could see the sky clearly in the city with all the background light. He was anxious to get on with the next step, but he was learning patience. It had been out there for billions of years—it would wait a few more days for him.

If it was a new comet, he would have the privilege of naming it. Probably that was why he had been whistling while cleaning his telescope. The weird thing was that when he had started building his new instrument, he had known he would find a comet.

He had also gone out for the basketball team. Their old coach had moved onto bigger things in the college ranks and their new coach was a bimbo, but Michael was having fun. Their first league game of the season would be a week from Friday. And the next game, the Friday after that, would be at home, right before the homecoming dance. It would be a good opportunity to show off his new jump shot.

Yet with all this new outlook on life, Michael had not given in to the common consensus that Alice McCoy had committed suicide. He could understand how others believed so, and he no longer blamed them for holding such a belief, but he was, if anything, more certain than ever that she had been murdered. Perhaps it was another intuitive conviction. Or maybe it was the product of dwelling too long on an idea that had come to haunt him:

Whoever had murdered once, could murder again.

Michael left his telescope in the garage and went into the kitchen. There was a call he had been meaning to make. Last night, while falling asleep, he suddenly remembered something very important about the way Alice had painted.

He dialed the police station, identified himself, and asked for Lieutenant Keller. He had not spoken to the detective since the day of the funeral.

"Mike," Keller said with a note of pleasure, but without surprise, when he came on the line. "How have you been?"

"Very well, sir, thank you. How are you?"

"Good. What can I do for you?"

"First I'd like to ask if there have been any new developments on the McCoy case?"

Keller paused. "I'm afraid not, Mike. As far as this department is concerned, Alice McCoy's death has officially been ruled a suicide."

The news was not unexpected, but nevertheless disappointing. "Does that mean you've completely closed the book on the matter? I think I might have another lead.''

"Did you obtain the full name of that boyfriend of Alice's you mentioned?''

"No, I haven't. No one seems to know anything about him. But I haven't given up trying. I think long enough has gone by that I can talk directly to Alice's sister, Polly, about the guy.''

"Sounds like a good idea." Keller was being polite, that was all. Michael knew he still thought he was dealing with a distraught teenager. It bothered Michael, but not that much. "What's your lead?''

"Do you have a CRT on your desk?" Michael asked.

"Yes.''

"Can you access the autopsy report on Alice McCoy?''

"Yes, but as I've already explained, I cannot divulge that information without written permission from the family.''

"I understand. But I'm not asking you to let me look at it right now, I'm just asking you to look at it.''

Keller chewed on that a moment. He seemed to sigh beneath his breath. "Hold a minute and I'll punch up the record." Michael listened as the detective tapped on a keyboard. It took Keller three or four minutes to get to the autopsy, an unusually long time. He was probably rereading it first. Finally he said, "I'm looking at it.''

"Who performed it?''

"I told you, I can't—''

"How can the doctor's name be confidential?" Michael interrupted. "The list of the city's coroners is public knowledge." Poor logic, but his tone was persuasive. Keller admitted something significant.

"As a matter of fact the autopsy wasn't performed by a city coroner, but by a paid consultant.''

"Why?"

"Our own people were probably busy at the time. Look, if it will make you happy, the gentleman's name was Dr. Gin Kawati."

Michael jotted down the information. "Do you know his phone number?"

"Mike—"

"All right, never mind. But let me ask you something else. You said that Alice's, Nick's, and Kats's fingerprints were all on the gun. Is that correct?"

"Yes."

"Does the report state which hand the fingerprints were from?"

"It does."

"Which hand was Alice holding the gun in?"

"You were there. She had it in her right hand."

"Were any fingerprints from her left hand on the gun?"

"Not that I can tell from this report. What's your point?"

"Alice McCoy was left-handed."

Again Keller paused. "Are you sure?"

"Yeah. I remembered last night how she used to paint. She always held the brush in her left hand. Interesting, don't you think?"

Keller sounded slightly off balance. "Yes, yes, it is. But it doesn't prove anything. She could just as well have held the gun in her right hand and put it in her mouth."

"Are you right-handed, Lieutenant?"

"I am, yes."

"If you were going to kill yourself, which hand would you hold your gun in?"

"What kind of question is that?"

"I know it sounds morbid," Michael said quickly. "But think about it for a moment. Even if a girl is about to commit suicide, she would still handle the gun carefully. She would be worried about getting off a clean shot, of doing it right the first time. She would be nervous. She wouldn't hold the thing in her weak hand."

"Now you're getting into the psychology of someone suffering from depression. For all either of us knows, she could have intentionally done everything backward."

"She wasn't depressed!" Michael snapped, before catching himself. "When you go home tonight, think about it for a while. That's all I ask."

"All right, Mike, I'll do that. Anything else?"

"Yeah. Could I swing by and pick up that permission form you keep saying I need?"

"I have to go in a few minutes, but I can leave it at the front desk for you."

"I'd appreciate that. One last thing. Was Alice's right hand dusted for prints?"

"I can't tell from this report. But during the party, she could have shook hands with any number of people. Such prints would have been meaningless."

"I wonder," Michael said.

They said their good-byes, both sides promising to be in touch. It was four o'clock; the sun set early this time of year. Michael dialed a number that gave up-to-the-minute weather reports. The word was that it would be raining again in the desert. He decided to finish cleaning his telescope and put it away.

The garage was somewhat stuffy. He pushed open the door, deeply breathing the crisp evening air. It was then he noticed the car parked up the street.

Michael had never seen Jessica leave school in her car, but he remembered the silver-blue Celica in her driveway the evening of their date. This car appeared to be the identical make, and someone was sitting in the front seat. Because of the lighting, however, he couldn't tell who it was, whether it was a male or a female even. Well, he had just the thing to solve the mystery.

He positioned his telescope in the driveway behind a bush. With a little maneuvering, he was able to see the person between the branches without being seen. A moment of focusing presented him with a clear view of every detail on Jessica Hart's face.

She was working on something and had a pencil in her mouth. He watched for a minute while she scratched her head, wrinkled her forehead, glanced at her watch, and grimaced. No matter what the expression, to him she was beautiful.

Since he had returned to school, he had gone to great pains to avoid her, more than he had during the week following their one date. He'd asked and received another locker. He'd avoided the courtyard during both break and lunch. He'd obtained a list of her classes from the computer at school and mapped out in his head where she should be at any particular moment, planning his own routes accordingly.

"I loved Alice. I loved her more than the world. And what I said to the police, I didn't say because I wanted to. It hurt me to say it, as much as it's hurting me to stand here and have you accuse me. . . ."

Naturally, despite his precautions, he had occasionally bumped into her, anyway. But they'd exchanged few words. Hello. How are you? Take care. Good-bye. But he'd seen enough of her to know his longing for her had not died with Alice, as he had thought it would. It had only grown stronger.

She was parked in front of Julie Pickering's house. He hadn't realized they were friends. She was probably waiting for Julie to come home. From what he could see, he guessed she might be finishing up some homework before knocking on Julie's door. She could disappear any second.

He didn't give himself a chance to think about it, to

chicken out. He started up the street. He had decided that first night in the desert that he owed her an apology.

Halfway to her car, he saw her notice him. He waved.

"Hi. Jessie?"

She rolled down her window, peeked her head outside, her long brown hair covering her shoulder. "Yeah, it's me," she said, her smile strained. "Hi, Michael. I guess you're wondering what I'm doing here?"

He nodded toward the Pickerings' residence. "You know Julie, don't you?"

Jessica glanced at Julie's house. "Ah, yeah, Julie. Yeah, I know her."

"Are you two going to study together?" He remembered Julie, like Jessica, was taking chemistry.

"Yeah, that's it. I mean, I didn't know you and Julie lived on the same block?"

He gestured vaguely back the way he had come. "I live over there."

"Oh."

He put his hands in his pockets, looked at the ground. That was the neat thing about the ground. It was always there to look at when you were talking to a pretty girl. He didn't know how to begin.

"I haven't seen you around school much," she said finally.

"I've been around."

"Do you have a new locker?"

"Yeah, they gave me one. Somebody transferred to another school." He shrugged. "It was available."

"I bet you have a lot more room now?"

"You never crowded me."

"Sure I did. With my bag and my makeup and stuff. I don't know how you put up with me."

"I was the one who ruined your sweater."

"You didn't ruin it."

"Yeah, I did."

"No." She reached out, brushed his arm. "Look at me, Michael." He did so, seeing her large brown eyes first, as he usually did when he looked at her. She chuckled. "Don't you see? I have it on."

He smiled. "That's right. How did you get the stain out?"

She touched her chest. "I don't remember. It doesn't matter. It's gone."

"It looks great on you."

"Thank you." She paused, her face suddenly serious. "Did you ask for a new locker?"

He couldn't lie to her. "Yeah."

The word seemed to startle her. She recovered quickly, however, nodding. "That's OK."

"Jessie—"

"No, I understand. It's fine, really, no offense taken. It's just that I sort of, you know—I used to like talking to you between classes." She smiled briefly. "That was fun."

"I'm sorry," he said.

"It's all right."

"No, I'm sorry about what I said to you." He lowered his voice, his eyes. "When we were in Alice's studio. I shouldn't have said—what I did."

She sank back into her seat, taking a breath, putting her hands on the steering wheel, pulling them off again. Obviously, it was a topic she would have preferred to avoid. "You were upset," she said quietly.

"I was an asshole."

She started to shake her head, stopped. She could have been talking about the stain again. "I don't remember what you said. It doesn't matter, anyway. It's past."

"Do you forgive me?"

"I don't have to forgive you for loving her." She

27

caught his eye. "That's all I heard in that room, Michael—that you loved her. All right?"

She did forgive him, and she was asking him to drop it. "All right," he said, feeling much better. He should have come to her weeks ago. She picked up her papers and books from the passenger seat, glad to change the subject.

"You can see I'm still studying for the SAT," she said. "I have to take it, not this Saturday, but next."

"That's when I'm taking it. At Sanders High?"

She brightened. "Yeah. Maybe we'll be in the same room."

"Maybe."

She nodded to her test book. "I'm not doing so hot on these trial tests. How do you score on them?"

He had not given a thought to the SAT. "I haven't taken any."

"Really? You're just going to walk in there and do it? That's amazing." She glanced at her scratch papers, frowned. "I wish I could do that."

"You'll do fine. Don't worry about it."

"I'm not worried." She laughed. "I'm terrified."

He smiled. "If worse comes to worst, I can always slip you my answers—if you'd want them."

She looked up at him. "Don't tempt me, guy."

"Of course you'd have to pay me in advance."

"Oh! I do have to pay you. I mean, I still owe you a movie." She paused. "Would you like to go to the movies with me?"

He felt much much better. "When?"

"How about tomorrow?"

Tomorrow was Friday, and he *had* to work because he was already taking Saturday off to play in the final practice game of the season. He couldn't do that to his bosses—disappear two days in a row during the busiest part of the week. They'd already given him a break by not firing him when he had stayed at home for days on end after the funeral.

On the other hand, this last preseason game was against a marshmallow of a school. And Coach Sellers was still trying to make up his mind about a couple of guards. If he did call in sick, the team would still win, and the two guys would get more playing time, and have more of an opportunity to prove themselves. By working Saturday, he could rationalize taking Friday off.

"Tomorrow would be great," he said.

They worked out the details. He would pick her up at six at her house and they would take it from there. She squeezed his hand just before she drove away. He decided she had changed her mind about studying with Julie.

He didn't know what was the matter with him. He could never sit around and enjoy a happy moment. His brief conversation with Lieutenant Keller suddenly came back to plague him. He hadn't had enough information to challenge the detective. He needed more. He needed to study that autopsy report.

He got into his car, drove to the police station. There he picked up the permission form. The sooner he got it back to them, the sooner he might clear Alice's name. He headed for the McCoy residence.

Polly answered the door. There were shadows beneath her eyes, and the rest of her features looked drawn and tired. She had lost a great deal of weight, particularly in her face. He had never realized how pretty she was, or how much she resembled her sister.

"Hi, Mike," she said. She had on dark wine-colored pants, a white blouse, a red scarf around her neck. "How are you?"

"I'm all right. How about you?"

"Fine. Would you like to come in?"

"Yeah, thanks." He stepped inside, bracing himself

involuntarily. Even twenty years from now he doubted that he would feel comfortable in this mansion. The plush carpet, the high white ceilings—he remembered it all too well. There was, however, a slight stale odor in the air he did not recall. Polly led him toward the couch in the living room where he'd been sitting with Nick and Maria when the gun had gone off.

"I was in the neighborhood, and I thought I'd stop by and see how things are," he said as they sat down.

"That was nice of you."

He glanced about. "It's amazing how neat you're able to keep this place."

"Polly." A thin voice sounded from the direction of the hallway. Polly immediately leaped to her feet, but stopped at the start of the hall.

"It's a friend from school, Aunty. Do you need anything?"

"No, dear, talk to your friend first."

"First? *Do* you need anything?"

"Go ahead and talk to your friend," the old woman said.

Polly shook her head, mildly irritated, and returned to her place beside Michael on the couch. "She'll probably call out again in a minute," she said.

"How is she? Someone told me she'd had a heart attack?"

She nodded. "Yeah. The doctors say it was mild, but she's so old. She hasn't really got her strength back. She has to stay in the downstairs bedroom. The climb upstairs is too much for her."

"Do you have a nurse?"

"I can take care of her. If she'd tell me what she wants. She doesn't know half the time." Polly shook her head again and then looked at him, smiling, pain beneath the smile. He almost decided right then and there not to bring up the reason for his visit. "I'm glad

30

you stopped by," she said. "It gets kind of boring sitting home every night."

"You should try to get out."

Polly glanced toward the front hall, or was it up, toward the bedroom where they had found Alice. That was one room he'd like to look at again. "Not yet," she said.

He cleared his throat. "Polly, I have a confession to make. I did have another reason for stopping by. I have a few questions I want to ask you."

"Would you like something to eat?"

"No thanks. What I wanted—"

"How about something to drink?"

He smiled. "Sure. Juice would be nice."

She jumped up. "What flavor? We have pineapple-coconut?"

"That would be fine."

She was back in a minute with a huge ice-filled glass, a slice of orange stuck on the rim. She hadn't bothered about one for herself. She sat on the couch a little closer this time, her expression now more alert than hurt. "Is it good?" she asked.

He took a sip. "Great." He set it in his lap, stirred the ice with the straw she had provided. "I wanted to ask about Alice," he said carefully.

"We can talk about her," she said quickly. "Jessie and Sara—they think I'll break down if I hear her name. But I won't. She was my sister, after all, why shouldn't I talk about her?"

"That's a good attitude." Man, this was hard. Despite what she said, he felt as if he were treading on thin ice on a hot day. "What I wanted to say— Do you think Alice killed herself?"

"Didn't she?"

"Do *you* think she did?"

Polly turned her head away, stared off into space for a moment. "What?"

Michael set down his drink on the coffee table. "Do you think she was the suicidal type?"

She frowned. "Do you mean before she killed herself? She only killed herself the one time. At least that was the only time she tried, that I know of."

"Do you think there might have been other times?"

"She never told me about any other time. She didn't tell me about this time, before she did it I mean. But she didn't always tell me everything. We were close, but she had her secrets, which I think is all right."

"Polly."

"What? Did I put too much ice in your juice?"

"No. What I'm trying to say is I don't think she killed herself."

"No?"

"No. I think she was murdered."

Polly was impressed, to a certain extent. "Really?"

"Yes."

"Who murdered her?"

"I don't know. That's why I'm here. I'm trying to find out."

Polly was suddenly confused. "You don't think I did it, do you?"

"No."

She relaxed. "I didn't. I thought she did it. That's what that doctor at the hospital told me. The man with the electricity."

"The man with the what?"

Polly shook her head. "Never mind. I see what you're saying. You think someone killed her on purpose, and not accidentally."

"Yeah."

"And you don't know who it is?"

"Right." He sat up, folded his hands. "Polly, just before Alice died, you went outside to check the chlorine in the pool. Do you remember if you turned the pool light off?"

She nodded. "Sure I remember. I have a good memory. I turned it off."

"After you put the chlorine in the water?"

"Yes."

"How long before you heard the shot did you turn off the light?"

"Not long."

"A minute?"

"Yeah."

That would explain why the room had been so dark. "When you were outside at the pool, did you see anybody?"

"No."

"Did you hear anything? Like up on the roof?"

"No."

"Are you sure?"

"No. Yes."

"What did you do when you heard the shot?"

"Wh— I came inside. You saw me. Don't you remember?"

"I remember." She had been about to say something else. "Tell me about Clark?"

Polly spoke defensively. "I don't know his last name."

"I understand. But can you tell me anything about him? How did you meet him?"

"On a hike in the mountains. I sprained my ankle and he came and drew my picture."

"Where in the mountains?"

"I don't know what the place is called. We took that road that leads up and away from the racetrack."

"The Santa Anita Racetrack?"

"Yeah, we went up there."

"You and Alice?"

"Yeah."

"What school did Clark go to?"

"I don't know if he went to school."

"But wasn't he our age?"

"I don't know. He never talked about school. Alice told me you met him?"

"I did, yeah, at the first football game. Tell me, what did he talk about?"

"Weird stuff. He was a weird guy. But he—he was interesting, too."

"Why did Alice go out with him?"

"He was an artist. He was showing her all kinds of far-out techniques, opening her up."

"Were they romantically involved?"

Polly's face darkened. "What do you mean?"

He had to keep in mind Polly had gone out with Clark before Alice. "Were they boyfriend and girlfriend?"

"You mean, did they sleep together? Of course they didn't. Do you think I would let my little sister have sex with someone like that? I was the one who told Alice not to invite him to the party. If she was here, she would tell you that."

Michael stopped, feeling a chill at the base of his spine. "Did Clark come to the party?"

"What?"

"Was Clark at the party?"

"I told you, I told Alice not to invite him."

"But did he come? Without being invited?"

"He wouldn't have come without an invitation. He was weird, but he wasn't weird like that."

"But—"

"Polly," the aunt called.

Groaning, Polly got up. "Coming," she said, disappearing down the hall off the central foyer. She reappeared a moment later. "I'm sorry, Mike. I can't talk anymore. I have to—take care of her. I'm really sorry."

He stood up, pulling the permission form from his back pocket. "That's OK, I shouldn't have barged in on you like this, anyway. Maybe we can talk about this some other time?"

"Sure."

"Hey, could I ask a big favor? You see this paper? It's a legal document that gives me permission to review the report that was done on your sister."

"What report?"

He hated to use the word. "The autopsy report."

She accepted the sheet, glanced at it. "You want me to sign it?"

"No, I want your aunt to sign it. She was Alice's legal guardian."

"But why?"

"I feel there may be something in the report that the police overlooked."

Polly folded the form. "I'll ask her to look at it."

"I'd really appreciate it. Another thing. Could you please keep this visit between us private? Don't talk to Jessie or Sara about it? They think—I don't know, that I should just drop the whole thing."

Polly nodded sympathetically. "They're like that a lot of the time."

She showed him to the door. As he was stepping outside, she put her hand on his arm, looked up at him. Again, the pain behind her eyes was all too clear, and he wondered if he'd added to it with his questions. She seemed to read his mind, as Alice used to do.

"I don't mind talking to you about how she died," she said. "She always told me what a great person you were. She told me I could trust you."

Michael smiled uncomfortably. "That was nice of her."

She continued to hold on to him. "Don't go after Clark, Mike. Alice told me about him, too. The night she died— She said he was no good."

"Are you saying he might hurt me?"

"I don't know. I don't want you to get hurt."

"Was he at the party, Polly?"

Now she let go of him, raising her hand to her head, trembling ever so slightly. "I don't remember," she said softly. "There were so many people there. Too many uninvited people."

He patted her on the shoulder, thanked her again for her help. Climbing into his car, he felt vaguely disoriented. If she hadn't loved Alice so much, and if he hadn't seen her go out to the pool immediately before the shooting, he would have added Polly to his list of suspects.

"That's what the doctor at the hospital told me. The man with the electricity."

CHAPTER FOUR

It was later. Michael was gone, her aunt was sleeping, and the sun had gone down. Polly sat alone in the dark, the TV on, the sound off. She preferred it that way, watching people she didn't have to listen to. Sometimes at school she felt as if she would go mad, all those people talking all the time. Even her best friends, Jessica and Sara, they never shut up. And whenever she had something to say, they were too busy to listen.

Polly reached for another carrot. She had read that eating a lot of carrots improved your ability to see in the dark. Since she spent most nights awake answering her aunt's calls, it was important to her. Besides, carrots helped you lose weight. That's what Alice used to say. And look how skinny Alice had been. Thin as a stick.

She wasn't sure what she was watching, some stupid sitcom. Practically everything on TV these days was stupid. She didn't know if many people realized it, but the networks were even beginning to rerun the news.

Polly sat up suddenly. What was that sound? She had heard a banging noise. It seemed to be coming from out back. She hoped it was a cat. She was terrified of burglars. She didn't have a gun in the house, only her dad's old shotgun, which she couldn't even find. Getting up, she peeked through the drapes covering the sliding-glass door.

There was nobody there, at least nobody she could see. But with the approaching storm, it was unusually dark outside. She stood still for a moment, listening to the wind, the rustling of the trees. The noise was probably nothing but a branch knocking against the outside wall. There was probably no need to call the police.

Oh!

A bolt of white light split the sky, causing her to jump. Instinctively, she started to count, as she had been taught as a child. The crack of thunder hit between two and three. The rain followed almost immediately, pelting the pool water like sand particles blasting a windshield. Like sometimes happened in the desert when a car went off the road.

Polly bowed her head, leaning it on the glass door. All of a sudden she missed her parents, missed them real bad. *Their* car had gone off the road, right into a ditch, where it had exploded. She had been small at the time, but she remembered exactly how it had happened. There had been an argument about something, and then the car was burning and the doctor was telling her everything was all right. She didn't understand why doctors always lied.

"The wires won't hurt. You won't even feel them."

But she felt everything. Liars.

Polly walked upstairs, headed down the hall, and turned right, entering the last room on the left, her parents' bedroom and the room where Alice had died. The chalk outline the police had drawn had been washed away long before she had returned to the house after her sister's death, but she could still distinguish a trace of it on the hard wooden floor—even in the dark. Sometimes, when she felt sad as she did now, she found it soothing to come into this room and rest on the spot where they had found Alice. Stretching out on the floor, she lay with her eyes open, staring at the ceiling.

Lightning flashed, thunder rolled. The gaps between the two seemed to lengthen. But the rain kept falling, and the storm was not going away. She noticed that the time between her breaths was also growing. She counted ten seconds between inhaling and exhaling, then fifteen. She wondered if her heart was slowing down. Lying there, she often felt as if she understood what it had been like for Alice when they had found her on the floor. It hadn't been so bad. The dead might bleed, but they never cried.

Polly realized she was crying. It was all because she was alive. They had all gone and left her alone. A wave of despair pressed down on her, but she fought it, fighting to sit up. They hadn't cared about her. They hadn't asked what she wanted with her life. Her dad had decided to drive off the road. Her mom had gone ahead and burned. And Alice had taken that stupid gun and—

No!

Polly leaped to her feet. That banging sound again. Only now it was coming from outside the window. She crept to the shades, lifted it, and peered down, seeing nothing at first but the garden, the rainy night. Then there was another flash of lightning. And there he was! Someone in her backyard!

"Hey, you! What are you doing there?"

The sound of her voice didn't cause him to run away, nor did it startle him. He cupped a hand over his eyes, looking up, his long scraggly hair hanging over his shoulders. She took a step away from the window, her heart hammering. She should have kept her mouth shut, she thought, and called the police. But then he spoke.

"Is that you, Polly?"

Relief flushed through her, followed by a fear of a different sort. "Clark? What are you doing down there?"

"Trying to get in. It's wet out here. I rang the front doorbell a dozen times. Why didn't you answer?"

"The front doorbell doesn't work." It had broken the night of the party.

"I knocked, too."

"I'm sorry, I thought— I don't know. Just a sec. Go around to the back patio. I'll let you in."

He had on the black leather jacket and pants he wore on his motorcycle. For the most part, the rain had left him untouched. Except for his tangled red hair. Soaked, it seemed much darker.

"I was beginning to believe you'd left this big box to the ghosts," he said as she slid open the sliding-glass door that led out onto the roof-covered patio. "How are you, babe? Been a long time."

"Yeah, months. I can't believe you're here. Why didn't you call before coming?"

He wiped at his pale face with his long bony fingers. He had always been skinny. Now he was close to emaciated. "I wanted to see you, I didn't want to talk to you." He grinned. "You look exotic, Polly, real tender."

She beamed, relaxing a notch. She didn't know why she had felt she had to warn Michael away from Clark. Why, here he was right in front of her and everything

39

was cool. "Thanks, you look nice, too. Do you want to come in?"

"Nah," he said, nodding to his mud-caked boots. "Better not. Don't want to spoil the scene. Like to keep pretty things pretty." He turned toward the side of the house where she had first seen him, and the grin seemed to melt from his face as if he were a clay sculpture in the rain. His entire manner changed. "Why didn't you tell me?" he said.

She bit her lip. "I thought you knew."

He looked at her, his green eyes darkening. "I didn't know until I read about the funeral in the papers."

"Did you go?"

"You know I didn't."

"I didn't know. They had me in the hospital."

He was angry. "But I called. I left messages."

"The machine was acting up. I didn't get them."

He shook his head, stepping away from the door, turning his back to her, reaching his palm out from beneath the shelter of the patio. The rain continued to pour down. "Who killed her?" he asked.

"The police say it was a suicide."

He thought about that a moment, then his mood changed again, and he chuckled. "The police. What else do they say?"

"Nothing."

"Did they ask about me?"

She hesitated. "They didn't."

He whirled. "Did someone else?"

She had never been able to lie to him. He had some kind of power over her she didn't understand. "A boy at school."

"What's his name?"

"Michael."

"What's his last name?"

"I'm—not sure." She added weakly, "He wanted to know your last name."

He moved to her, briefly touched her chin with his wet fingers, and it was almost as if an electrical current ran through his nails; she couldn't help quivering. "Remember when we met?" he asked. "On that sacred ground? The Indians buried there believed if you knew a person's secret name, you could make him do anything you wished. Anything at all."

"Is that why you never told me your full name?"

He grinned again. "Do you believe that nonsense?"

"No."

He held her eyes a moment. "I remember this Michael. I met him at the football game. Do you know if he saw me at the party?"

Lightning cracked again, thunder roared, the smell of ozone filling the air. Polly put a hand to her head, rubbed her temple. She didn't feel pain, only a slight pressure and immense surprise. "You were at the party?" she said.

"Yeah, I came at the end like you told me to. Don't you remember?"

"Yeah," she said quickly. "I had just forgotten for a moment, that's all." She really did remember, not everything maybe, but a lot. The three of them had been in the room together. They had gotten into an argument about the paper cups, or why Clark hadn't come earlier, something like that. Then she and Clark had left Alice alone in the room and gone downstairs. He had left on his motorcycle and she had gone out the back to check on the chlorine in the pool. Then Alice had gone for the gun. . . .

The loneliness Polly had experienced in the bedroom suddenly crashed down upon her, and she burst out crying. Clark's wet arms went around her, and she leaned into them.

"All I did was fight with Alice and make her think I

hated her when I loved her more than I loved anything,'' she said. ''And now she's gone, and Aunty's
here, but she can hardly breathe. Help me, Clark,
you've got to help me. I can't live like this. I feel I
have to die.''

He didn't say anything for the longest time, just held
her as he used to hold her before he had started to see
Alice. When he finally did release her, she felt a little
better, though slightly nauseated. He brushed the hair
from her eyes, accidentally scratching her forehead
with one of his nails.

''You'll be all right, kid,'' he said. ''You don't have
to die. You didn't do nothing wrong. Nothing at all.''

''But I—''

''Shh. Enough tears. Mourn too much and you
disturb the sleep of the dead. Tell me, does Michael
say Alice was murdered?''

She dabbed her eyes. ''He's suspicious.''

''Hmm. What else?''

''He gave me a paper he wants Aunty to sign.''

''Show it to me.''

He barely glanced at the form when she handed it
over, folding it and sticking it in his coat pocket. ''I'll
look at it later,'' he said.

''If you want, I can read it to you now. I've been
eating lots of carrots. I can see in the dark.''

He brushed aside her comment, sticking his head in
the doorway, sniffing the air. ''It stinks in this place.
That old lady's still here?''

''Yeah. She's sick. She had a heart attack. I take
care of her.''

''Why? Old people—when their number's up, they
die. It doesn't matter what you do.''

''Don't say that!''

''That's reality, babe. Sometimes they choke to
death on their tongues. It's a hassle watching her all
the time, isn't it?''

"I don't mind. I take good care of her."

He grinned and started to speak again just as someone knocked at the front door. "Who's that?" he snapped.

"I don't know. I'll go see."

"No, wait, I'll go. My bike's parked at the end of your driveway beneath that ugly tree, but it's probably getting wet." He grabbed her by the arm, pulled her toward him. She thought for a moment he was going to kiss her, but then he let her go, gesturing for her to follow him away from the patio. "Come here."

"Out in the rain? I'll get wet."

"Who cares?"

She walked over and stood beside him in the downpour. The person at the front door knocked again. She hardly noticed. The water felt delicious atop her head, the drops sliding down inside her blouse and over her breasts. Clark took her into his arms again, leaned close to her ear. "I like you this way," he whispered. "Cold, like me." He kissed her neck lightly, and she could imagine how the rain must have drenched deep into his flesh while he had raced through the night on his motorcycle; his lips sent a chill into her blood, a warmth up her spine. "Do you love me, Polly?"

"I-I'm glad you're here."

"Do you want me to come again?"

"I do."

"Then I will." He kissed her again on the neck, took a step back. "I have a secret to tell. Can you keep a secret?"

"Sure."

"First you must promise not to talk about me to anybody." He scratched her shoulder lightly, pinching the material. "You must cross your heart and hope to die."

She sketched a cross over her chest. "I promise. What is it?"

"Michael knows something. But what he knows, he knows it backward. Alice didn't kill herself."

"How do you know?"

"Your sister was too cute to wash her hair with her own blood."

"Who did kill her?"

He stared at her with his bright green eyes. The person at the front door knocked a third time. "You don't know?"

"No."

"Would you lie to me?"

She began to feel a bit sick again. "I honestly don't know."

His face softened with a sympathy she had never seen in him before. "Maybe I can't remember, either. But I paint what I see. Listen closely and ponder deeply. It wasn't you who killed her, and it wasn't me who pulled the trigger."

She smiled at the absurdity of the idea. "Well, of course we didn't."

He turned to leave, spat on the grass. "Stay alive, babe, and stay cold. It's the only way for the likes of us."

He disappeared around the west side of the house, in the direction of the gate. He was such an interesting guy, she thought. She hurried to answer the door.

It was Russ. All he had on was a green T-shirt and blue jeans. Someone had punched him in the eye. The swelling reached to his nose. It was absolutely cool he had come over to see her messed up the way he was. "I need a place to stay," he said.

She had always known he liked her. Suddenly she was quite happy, and not the least bit lonely. All these nice boys wanting to talk to her and kiss her. It should rain more often.

But Clark might not like Russ kissing her. She could see his motorcycle at the end of the long driveway.

Her eyes darted toward the side of the house. He probably hadn't even gotten past the gate yet. She reached out, taking Russ by the arm, pulling him inside. "You poor dear," she said. "Let me make you dinner and you can tell me all about it."

She cooked him a steak and fries. There wasn't any beer in the house, but he seemed to enjoy the expensive bottle of French wine she fetched from her aunt's closet. He finished it off before getting to dessert. When she asked who had belted him, he just shrugged, which was OK with her. She wasn't the nosy type, not like a lot of people she knew.

They watched TV. He liked the old "Star Trek" reruns—with the sound on. They talked a little, but then he started to yawn. She led him upstairs to her own bedroom. He was such a gentleman, he didn't expect her to put out right away. He just said good night and closed the door. She crashed on the couch downstairs.

Her aunt kept her up half the night. She didn't mind. It was nice having a man in the house.

CHAPTER FIVE

Ηow could you be so careless?" Jessica asked.

"I took it into the store because I was trying to be careful," Sara said.

"Leaving a purse stuffed with three grand sitting in a supermarket freezer isn't my idea of being careful," Jessica said.

"I didn't just leave it. I set it down and then he chased me out of the place."

First period would begin in minutes. Jessica and Sara were in the parking lot, sitting in Jessica's car. Sara had let Jessica drive all the way to school before admitting she'd lost the majority of the ASB council's money.

"Russ chased you out of the freezer?" Jessica snorted. "More likely you locked him in the freezer. What did you find when you went back last night?"

"Well . . ."

"Did you find your bag?"

"Yes."

"With all the money gone?"

"Yes."

Jessica studied her old friend, suspicious. "What else?"

"The freezer door was gone, too."

"What happened to it?"

"The store manager says Russ chopped it down."

"*What?* You did lock him in! What the hell got into— Never mind. I don't want to know. Was Russ there when you went back?"

"No. His boss fired him for ruining the door."

"Did you explain that it was your fault?"

"No. I was trying to get my money back. I didn't want the boss mad at me."

"Man, you are dumb. You are the dumbest president I have ever seen."

"I was hoping you would cheer me up."

"You don't deserve it." They sat in silence for a moment. "He must have taken it," Jessica said finally. Sara only shook her head. "But you tried to turn him into a Popsicle. Why wouldn't he have taken it in revenge?"

"Russ wouldn't do that."

"Have you spoken to him?"

"I called his house."

"And?"

"He isn't living there anymore."

"Great. Fabulous. What are you saying?"

"His old man kicked him out. I don't know where he is." Sara scratched her head. "After Russ got fired, a half-dozen people ran in and out of that freezer for a couple of hours. They were moving all the frozen goods to another store so they wouldn't spoil. One of them must have found the bag, and stolen the money."

"A half-dozen employees shouldn't be that hard to check out."

"Oh, yeah."

Jessica drummed her fingers impatiently on the dashboard. "You've screwed up everything. You won't be able to afford the band. You won't be able to pay for the food. Homecoming will have to be postponed again. It'll probably be called off."

"And your crown might start to rust."

"That's not what I'm talking about."

"The hell it isn't! I'm in trouble, Jessie. And all you care about is winning some horse-faced beauty pageant!"

"That's not true!"

"It's all you think about!"

"So! What do you want me to do?"

"Give me some moral support! Quit telling me how dumb I am!"

"You are dumb! You go in to buy a can of Spam and find a date and you end up spending three grand and almost killing a guy!"

Sara gave her a weird look and sat back in the car seat. "You've made your point," she muttered.

Jessica took a deep breath. "I still think Russ must have taken it. I would have taken it."

Sara sighed. "No. I know him. He's not that kind of person. The money's gone, and it's gone for good."

"How much is left in the account?"

"About two thousand. But half of that will be eaten

47

up by checks I've already written.'' She shook her head. ''There isn't going to be enough.''

''How about hitting up Polly?''

''I tried that already. I talked to her this morning. She says she needs her aunt's signature to get hold of that much cash.'' Sara shrugged. ''I believe her.''

''Could you find another car to raffle?''

''There isn't time.'' Sara gave a miserable smile. ''I'm open to suggestions?''

Jessica thought a moment. ''I don't have any.''

The varsity tree was at both the physical and social center of Tabb High. A huge thick-branched oak, it stood halfway between the administration building and the library, near the snack bar. At lunch, without fail, at least half the jocks would gather under it to enjoy the good looks of half the girls on the pep squads. For the most part, except for the week before the party when she had been vigorously pursuing Bill Skater, Jessica avoided the area. Crowds, even friendly ones, often tired her. But today was different. The results of the balloting to determine who would be on Tabb High's homecoming court would be announced from a platform set up beneath the tree.

''Where's Sara?'' Maria Gonzales asked. ''Isn't she going to read the names?''

''No, I hear Mr. Bark, my political science teacher, is playing MC,'' Jessica said. ''Sara's got a lot on her mind.''

Maria was sympathetic. ''It must be hard for her to keep track of everything.''

''Tell me about it.''

''Are you nervous?'' Maria asked.

''I feel like I'm waiting to be shot.''

Maria nodded to the crowd. ''You're the prettiest one here. Anyone can see that.''

''Anyone but me.'' Dr. Baron had been right about

the letters and the numbers on the board making more sense when she had her glasses on, but all morning she couldn't help feeling people were staring at her and thinking she looked like an encyclopedia. At the moment, however, she had her glasses in her hand, and for that reason, she wasn't sure if she was hallucinating when she saw the long-legged blonde sitting all alone on one of the benches that loosely surrounded the varsity tree. Jessica pointed to the girl. "Who is that?" she asked.

Maria frowned. "Clair Hilrey."

"What's she doing?"

"Nothing."

Glancing around, Jessica quickly slipped on her glasses. The cheerleader was indeed by herself, and if that wasn't extraordinary enough, she looked downright depressed. "I wonder what's the matter with her."

"She's probably worried she won't be on the court."

"Clair's got the self-confidence of a tidal wave. No, that's not it. Something's wrong." Jessica took off her glasses and hid them away. "Which reminds me. During chemistry this morning, *you* were looking pretty worried."

"I'm fine."

"Come on, Maria. Haven't we been friends long enough? You're not happy. What is it?"

Her tiny Hispanic friend shyly shook her head. "I'm happy."

"Are you still thinking about Nick?"

"No."

After Alice's party, when the police were running in and out of the McCoy residence and questioning them all, Maria's parents had suddenly appeared. When Jessica had called her mom to explain what had happened, she forgot to tell her not to call the Gonzaleses.

That had been a mistake. Mr. and Mrs. Gonzales didn't even know their daughter was at a party—and at two in the morning. And then Maria's parents arrived precisely when Bubba was telling a detective about the fight in the pool between The Rock and Nick. Of course Maria had played a vital role in that fight, which Bubba mentioned right in front of her parents. It took them no time at all to figure out that Maria had been dating Nick. And it didn't help that the police chose Nick—along with Russ and Kats—to detain for further questioning. Jessica didn't hear exactly what they said to Maria, but from a quick glance at their faces as they were leaving, Jessica knew it couldn't have been anything gentle.

Parental law was still in effect in Maria's family: For absolutely no reason was she to go near Nick Grutler.

"Liar," Jessica said. She knew Maria was still thinking about Nick.

Maria started to protest again, but stopped herself. "I wish I could choose what to think about," she said sadly.

"It'll work out. It usually does."

Maria had her doubts. "I can't even talk to him about it."

"Sure you can. Your parents won't know. Explain the situation to him."

"How can I say that because he's black, my mom and dad assume he murdered Alice?" She shook her head. "It's better if he thinks I don't like him anymore. It's simpler this way."

Mr. Bark climbed onto the platform. The crowd quieted. Jessica hoped he wouldn't give a speech. A minute more of this waiting and she would scream.

He gave a speech—fifteen minutes—about how wonderful it was to be a teenager and to be alive in such exciting times. Bless him, he even worked in the need for nuclear disarmament. Jessica ground her teeth. Finally he pulled out the envelope.

"And now, the new homecoming court," he said, excited, opening the list. "Princess number one is . . ."

Jessica—Jessica—Jessica—me—me—me.

Mr. Bark paused, perplexed. "There seems to be some mistake. There are supposed to be five girls on the court. . . ." He stepped away from the microphone, spoke quietly to Bubba for a moment. Bubba kept nodding his head no matter what the teacher seemed to ask. Finally Mr. Bark returned to the mike. "The vote has resulted in an unusual situation," he said. "There was a six-way tie for fifth place. It has, therefore, been decided that there will be only four girls on the court this year. They are: Clair Hilrey, Cindy Fosmeyer, Maria Gonzales, and Jessica Hart."

Maria dropped her books and pressed her fingers to her mouth. Jessica let out a totally involuntary scream. Then they hugged each other and laughed with tears in their eyes. It felt good, Jessica thought. It felt better than just about anything had ever felt in her whole life. She couldn't stop shaking.

"I can't believe it," Maria kept saying. "I can't believe it."

"We don't have to believe it." Jessica laughed. "We're living it!"

People they knew and didn't know gathered around to offer their congratulations. Cindy Fosmeyer was one of them. She had huge breasts and a big nose. Jessica gave her a kiss. Everything seemed to be happening so fast. Pats on the back, smiles, hugs, kisses. But none of them were from Polly or Sara, and Jessica had started to look for them when Bill Skater came up and shook her hand.

"I knew you'd get on the court," he said.

"If you knew, why didn't you tell me!" She giggled, giving him a quick hug, which took him by surprise.

"Well, Jessie, you didn't ask."

She felt brave. She felt like a tease. "So I didn't. So why don't you ask me something?"

Such boyish blue eyes. He gave her a sexy look—with his face, it was the only kind he could give—but his voice was hesitant. "Do you want to go out tonight?"

The icing on the cake. Maybe she'd get a scoop of ice cream later. "Absolutely!"

She was a princess. She had a prince. She gave him her number, another hug, and went to find her friends.

She accidentally bumped into Clair instead, in Sara's locker hall, far from the hustle and bustle. Clair was alone. She in fact *looked* lonely. But they shook hands and she offered Jessica her congratulations.

"Four little princesses," Clair said. "Sounds like a bad fairy tale, doesn't it?"

"It's amazing about that tie," Jessica said.

"I wasn't surprised. Is Maria a friend of yours?"

"Yeah."

"Give her my regards."

"I will." Jessica smiled. "Aren't you excited?"

Clair turned to dial the combination on her locker. "Ask me in a couple of weeks, when they call out my name during the dance."

So that's how it was. "Maybe you'll be asking me."

Clair paused, giving her the eye. And now she smiled, slow and sure. "You may as well know, dearie, I can't lose."

CHAPTER SIX

Unknown to Jessica, Sara had watched the announcement of the homecoming court. But she had shied away from congratulating her best friend for a couple of reasons. First, as she had told Jessica in the car that morning, she thought Jessica had become overly preoccupied with the whole queen business. Second, with the loss of the money and Russ's getting fired, she was in a rotten mood and was afraid she'd say something nasty just when Jessica was enjoying her high moment. The fact that these two reasons were contradictory didn't make any difference to Sara. In reality, she was happy for both Jessica and Maria, and not the least bit jealous. She wouldn't have wanted to be a princess for anything. Being ASB president was enough of a pain in the ass.

She needed money and she needed to get Russ's job back for him. She didn't know which troubled her more. She was still smarting from his comments. She liked to think she didn't care about being popular. She had always thought of herself as subtle. But if Russ honestly believed—and it didn't matter whether he was right or wrong (although he was most definitely wrong)—she was using her position of authority to seduce him, then maybe there was something lacking in her approach. It was a possibility.

He was not at school today. All right, she'd worry about him the next day. Big bucks and fat Bubba were what mattered now. She followed Bubba as he left the varsity tree after the announcement, watched him disappear into the computer-science room. It was general knowledge that Bubba dealt in the stock market, and after checking around campus, she found out that he did extremely well. He was, in fact, a genius when it came to turning a few dollars into a few thousand. Knocking on the computer-room door and turning the knob, she hoped he didn't charge for advice.

He was already at a terminal, typing a million words a minute on the keyboard. He dimmed the screen the instant she entered, but appeared happy to see her. He offered her a chair.

"What do you think of our new batch of princesses?" he asked.

"I was surprised Maria Gonzales and Cindy Fosmeyer were selected," she said. "Maria's probably the quietest girl in the school, and Cindy—she's not exactly the princess type."

"You mean she's a dog?"

"Yeah."

Bubba nodded. "But she does have big breasts, and those babies go a long way with half the votes in the school." He glanced at his blank screen. "She's always been one of my favorites." He seemed to think that was funny, smiling to himself. "What can I do for you, Ms. President?"

"I have a small problem. I've been told you might be able to help me with it."

He leaned back in his seat, apparently satisfied that it was his reputation that had brought her to him. "Is it a financial or a sexual problem?" he asked.

"You have a lot of nerve."

"I also have a big bank account, and a huge— Well, let's just say I am willing and able to help in either department."

"It's a financial problem."

"A pity."

"I need three grand, and I need it by next week."

"Why?"

"There'll be no homecoming unless I get it."

"Why?"

"What do you mean, why? I need it to pay for everything."

"Have you already spent the money from the car raffle?"

"No, not exactly."

"What happened to the money? Did you lose it?"

"I—yeah, I did."

"How did you lose it?"

"What difference does it make? I lost it!"

"If you lost it on a guy, then I would have to say you have both a sexual and a financial problem. I like to know what I'm dealing with before I invest my time." He picked up a pen. "Are you going out with Russ Desmond?"

"What business is it of yours? No, I am not going out with him. Look, can you help me or not? Because if you can't, I haven't eaten lunch yet."

"Where would you like to go for lunch?"

"What?"

"I'll buy you lunch. Where would you like to eat?"

She stood. "Nowhere. Thanks for your time."

She was at the door when Bubba stopped her with the line, "I can get you the money, maybe."

"How?"

"Come back here and sit down." She did as she was told. He put aside his pen, leaned toward her, studying her face. "You're cute, Sara."

"How?" she repeated.

He shrugged. "Does it matter? You should be asking what it's going to cost you."

"What is it going to cost me?"

"Sex."

She chuckled in disbelief. "What?"

"Sex."

"Are you crazy? Are you saying you'll pay me three grand for my body?"

He sat back, shook his head. "No offense meant, but I would have to be crazy to spend that much money to sleep with you, or any girl for that matter. No, I said I can *get* you the money. I didn't say I would *give* it to you."

"Where are you going to get it? From your own account?"

"No, most of my money is tied up." He thought a moment. "How much do you have left?"

"A grand."

He considered again. "Can you get to that money this afternoon?"

"Not without Bill Skater's countersignature on a check."

"Do you have a copy of something Bill has signed?"

"Yeah."

"Then you can fake his signature."

"No, I'm not that desperate. I see what you're driving at. You want me to turn over the thousand to you."

"You *are* that desperate or you wouldn't be here. And, yes, I'll need what you have."

"No way. What are you going to do with it?"

"Invest it."

"Can you invest money and get that big a profit that quickly?"

"In the commodities market, you can lay out a hundred dollars today and have five hundred tomorrow."

"But I've heard investing in commodities is the same as rolling dice."

"Not if you know what you're doing. But I only mentioned commodities as an example. I haven't decided exactly what I will do with the grand. I'll have to think about it."

She shook her head. "This sounds pretty thin to me. I told you, I need this money within a few days. If you're not willing to get it out of your personal investments, then I can't take you seriously."

He was amused. "I notice you haven't said anything about my demand for sexual favors?"

"What am I supposed to say? You were kidding, weren't you?"

"No."

She realized she was blushing, and that he could tell she was blushing. "But you need to triple whatever I give you in less than a week," she persisted. "Nobody in the world can guarantee they can do that."

"Nobody in the world can guarantee anything. But I do believe—in fact, I'm almost certain—I can do great things with your money. Now as far as your deadline is concerned . . ." He picked up his pen again, reached for a piece of paper. "Who do you owe?"

"Mainly the caterer and the band."

"I need their names and phone numbers. I'll arrange it so we can pay them later."

"They won't go for that."

"They will after they talk to me. Give me the information."

"Wait! Let me get this straight. I'm going to give you a thousand dollars, and in return you're going to take responsibility for all the homecoming bills?"

"What is this responsibility crap? I'll do the best I can. That's all a man can do."

She swallowed. "And when you pay everything off, I have to sleep with you?"

"Yes."

"How many times?"

"Once."

"Is that all?"

"When it's over, you'll wish there were a hundred times yet to come."

"But you've been through half the girls on campus. God only knows what diseases you have."

"My vast experience has only made me all the more careful. Trust me, Sara, I'll take exquisite care of you." He paused. "Have we got a deal?"

She grimaced. "Has anyone ever told you what a sleaze ball you are?"

Bubba threw back his head and laughed.

CHAPTER SEVEN

If anyone else had chased after him so long to do something he didn't want to do, Nick Grutler thought, he probably would have punched him in the nose by now. But he respected Michael, and he learned it paid to listen to him. Michael was trying to persuade him to go out for the basketball team.

They were near the end of a one-on-one game, playing on an outside court near the girls' baseball field. The storm the night before had left an occasional puddle for them to dodge, but the water was slowing neither of them down. School had ended about an hour earlier, and the varsity team's official after-school practice had been canceled. The new coach had wanted the gymnasium floor waxed, and Tabb High's most recent crop of janitors had never done it before—and probably shouldn't be allowed to do it again; at the rate they were going, the floor wouldn't be ready for the homecoming game.

Michael had asked Nick to hang around to help him

with his jump shot. Naturally they had ended up trying to show each other up. It was no contest. Nick was ahead forty-four to thirty in a fifty-point game. Michael had trouble stopping Nick because Nick was able to palm the ball with equal ease with either hand, hit three-quarters of his shots anywhere within a twenty-foot radius of the basket, and—according to Michael, although Nick thought he was exaggerating—fly.

"But if this new coach you guys have is such a jerk," Nick said, tossing the ball to Michael to take out of bounds, "why should I put myself out for him?"

"You won't be doing it for him," Michael said, wiping the sweat from his forehead. Nick admired Michael's gutsy determination, especially on defense, even though he knew if he really wanted, he could score on him every time. "You'll be playing for yourself."

"On a team sport? Sure you don't want to take a break?"

"I'm all right," Michael said, dribbling slowly in bounds. "I mean you don't know how talented you are. I bet you could average thirty points and twenty rebounds a game if the rest of us didn't get in your way." He paused, panting, his free hand propped on his hip. "Are you ready?"

"I'm ready."

Michael nodded, continuing to dribble at the top of the key. "You get that kind of stats over the first half of the season and you'll have every college recruiter in the area coming to watch you play. Have you ever thought about that, going to college?"

"I never thought of graduating from high school till I met you," Nick said, not exaggerating. It had been Michael who had gotten him into academics at Tabb. Michael had done it by forcing him to read one book, from cover to cover, each week. It had been quite a chore for Nick because initially he'd had to go over each page three or four times with a dictionary. But he had learned that Michael's belief that the key to success in school was a strong vocabulary was absolutely true. He had found that even in math he could figure out how to work the problems now that he could follow the examples. He had also learned he enjoyed reading—he especially liked war stories—and that he wasn't dumb. Indeed, Michael had told him not more than an hour earlier that only someone with a high IQ could quadruple his vocabulary in the space of two months.

Nick was going to look up the exact definition of IQ as soon as he got home.

"Would you like to go to college?" Michael asked.

"I don't know what I'd do there."

"You would go to classes as you do here. Only you'd be able to major in any subject you wanted." Michael stopped suddenly, let fly with a fifteen-foot jump shot. Nick sprang up effortlessly, purposely swatting it back in Michael's direction. "Nice block," Michael muttered, catching the ball.

"Do people major in history?" Nick asked.

"Sure. You enjoy reading about the past, don't you?"

"It's interesting to see how people used to do stuff." Michael appeared undecided what to do next. "Why don't we take a break?" Nick suggested.

"Only if you're tired?"

Nick yawned, nodded. A week after Alice McCoy's funeral, Michael had called him with a job lead at a vitamin-packing factory. Nick had immediately ridden to the place on his bike. He had been hired on the spot. Only later had he come to understand they'd taken him on as a favor to Michael. Apparently, Michael had once helped the owner's son—Nick didn't know all the details. He was just thankful to have cash coming in so his dad wouldn't throw him out. But the hours were long and there was a lot of heavy lifting. He usually worked swing—three to twelve. He couldn't imagine taking on the extra burden of daily basketball practice. He told Michael as much as they walked to the sidelines and collected their sweats.

"You shouldn't be working full-time," Michael said. "You're only in high school. Does your dad take all your money?"

"Just about."

"That's not fair."

"If you ever met my dad, and he wanted your paycheck, believe me, you'd give it to him. Anyway, *you* work full-time."

"That's different. My mom needs the dough. And that's beside the point. You've got to take the long-term perspective on this. Imagine—you go out for the team, blow everybody's mind, get offered a college scholarship, earn a degree, land a job where you don't have to kill yourself every day for the rest of your life, and you can see how it would be worth it to sacrifice a few hours of sleep for the next few months."

Nick wiped his brow with his sweatshirt, slipped it over his head. "Forget about psyching me up for a minute and tell me this: am I really that good?"

"You're better than that."

Nick shook his head. "I can't believe this." In response, Michael snapped the ball toward his face. "Hey!" he shouted, catching it an inch shy of the tip of his nose. "Watch it."

Michael nodded. "There isn't another kid in the school who could have caught that ball. The best somebody else might have done was knock it away. You've got reflexes. You've got hands. And you've got a four-foot vertical jump. Trust me, you're *that* good."

Nick lowered his head, dribbled the ball beside his worn-out sneakers; he'd had only one pair of shoes in the past three years. "The Rock and a couple of his football buddies are on the team," he said. "What kind of welcome are they going to give me?"

"Oh, they'll try to make you feel like dirt. Especially when you start bouncing the ball off the top of their heads every time you slam-dunk. But I can't believe you'd let *them* stop you?"

"It's not just them. It's—something else."

"What?"

"Somebody's out to get me, Mike."

"Who?"

Nick grabbed hold of the ball, squeezed it tight, feeling the strength in his hands, and the anger, deeper inside, that seemed to give fuel to his strength. Except for brief moments it was as if he had been angry all his life—or alone and unwanted. It was often hard for him to tell the feelings apart. "There's this guy who goes to school here—his name's Randy. I don't know his last name."

"What's he look like?"

"He's ugly. He's got dark hair, bushy red sideburns, and a beer gut. He looks older. You know who I'm talking about?"

"I've seen him. What's he doing to you?"

"He's trying to sell me drugs. I know that doesn't sound like a big deal, but he keeps on me, even after I've told him a half-dozen times I'm not interested. I think he's trying to set me up."

"That serious?"

"Yeah. This afternoon, when I went to my locker, I found a Baggie sitting on top of my books, and a note that said 'On the House.' The Baggie had a couple of grams of coke in it."

"What did you do with it?" Michael asked.

"I gave it to Bubba."

"What did you do that for?"

"He was with me when I found it. He wanted it."

"But Bubba doesn't do drugs."

"Maybe he wanted to sell it, I don't know."

Michael considered a bit. "The fact that he looks older could be important. It might be possible to use the computer to check on— Hey, what is it?"

She was coming out of the girls' shower room, her long black hair tied in a ponytail as it had been the day they first met. Although small and far away, for a second, she was all he could see. "It's Maria," Nick said.

Michael was not impressed. He thought Maria was a phony for dumping Nick simply because the police had detained him at the station after Alice McCoy's death. Michael didn't know about her overriding fear of calling attention to herself, of being found out for what she was—an illegal alien. But maybe the knowledge wouldn't have made any difference to Michael. Often it seemed a poor excuse to Nick, too. Yet there wasn't an hour that went by when Nick didn't think of her.

"She must be feeling like hot stuff being elected to the homecoming court and all," Michael said.

"Not Maria."

Michael glanced at him, then at Maria. "I shouldn't have said that."

Nick rolled the ball in his hands. He would pop it next; he knew he could make it explode. "It's driving me nuts."

"What do you want to do?"

"Talk to her. But she doesn't want to talk to me."

"Have you asked her why?"

"I've tried."

"Try again. Try now."

"No. No, I can't."

"You have a perfect excuse to approach her. You want to congratulate her on making the court. Here, give me the ball. I'll wait for you."

"Mike . . ."

"Go, before she's gone."

He went; he only needed a shove. She saw him coming and turned to wait. He took that as a positive sign.

It wasn't.

"Hi," he said. "How are you?"

She appeared so calm, he thought she must surely be able to see how he was trembling inside. Yet a closer look showed her calmness to be no deeper than the welcome in her expression. She had waited for him out of politeness, not because she wanted to.

"Good," she said. "And you?"

"Oh, I'm all sweaty." He nodded toward Michael, and the courts. "We're playing some basketball."

She nodded, solemn as the day they'd met, only more distant now, not nearly so comfortable. "I saw you. Say hello to Mike for me."

"I will." That sounded like a good-bye. "I hear you're a school princess. That must be exciting?"

Her mood brightened, a bit. "I still don't believe it. I didn't think anyone knew who I was."

"It didn't surprise me. I voted for you."

"You did, really?"

"Of course."

"Who else did you vote for?" She sounded genuinely curious.

"Jessica and Sara and that girl Bubba sees—Clair."

"That's only four people. You could vote for five."

"They were the only ones I wrote down."

She seemed happy, in that moment, standing there listening to his praise, probably replaying in her mind the afternoon's announcement. But it didn't last. She looked at the ground. "I've got to go."

The word just burst out of him. "Why?"

"Because, Nick, because—" She clasped her books to her chest, her head still down. "I have to."

"I see." Then he said something that had been on his mind since the cops had led him to the jail cell with Kats and Russ the night Alice McCoy had taken a bullet through the head. "Is it because I was running down the stairs after the gunshot?"

She jumped slightly. "No."

"You think I killed her."

She turned away. "No!"

"You're the only one who knew I was coming down those stairs." He stopped, and now a cold note entered his tone. "Or are you, Maria?"

Her back to him, she nodded slowly. "I'm the only one. But that doesn't matter. None of that matters." She glanced over her shoulder, her eyes dark, lonely. "I have to go."

He shrugged. "Go."

When he returned to the court, Michael asked him how it had gone. Nick repeated everything that had been said, except the bit about his running down the stairs. It wasn't that he didn't trust Michael, he simply felt guilty for having lied to him after the funeral when they had originally discussed the matter. Back then, after having spent a few days in the slammer, he'd been afraid to say anything even remotely incriminating.

He needed respect, not just from Michael, but from everyone in school. Then maybe Maria would see him as something other than a threat. As they walked toward the showers, he said, "I think I will go out for the team."

CHAPTER EIGHT

Although he had been badly beaten on the court, Michael felt better for the exercise. The thought of his date that evening with Jessica wasn't slowing him down, either. He'd had trouble falling asleep the night before thinking about it.

After saying good-bye to Nick, Michael headed for the computer-science room. He'd been meaning to have a talk with Bubba. He decided now would be a good time.

Michael had not purposely avoided his old friend after Alice's death the way he had avoided Jessica, yet since then, he had spoken to Bubba very few times. He suspected Bubba may have been keeping his distance. Whatever the reason, it was time to clear the air between them.

On the way to Bubba, he passed a pay phone and thought of the form he'd given Polly. She hadn't been at school that day. He decided to give her a quick call. She didn't answer till the seventh or eighth ring.

"You barely caught me, Mike. I'm on my way out."

"I won't keep you then. I was wondering if I could swing by this afternoon and pick up that form I left last night?"

"What form?"

"The permission form I wanted your aunt to sign. Did she have a chance to read it over?"

Polly hesitated. "I don't know. I don't think so."

"Is there a problem? If you'd like, I could explain what it's for to your aunt."

66

"No, you don't have to do that."

"Do you have any idea when I could pick it up?"

"I'll see. I'll get back to you, all right?"

"Sure. I'll talk to you later."

Putting down the phone, he knew he'd wait a long time before Polly McCoy contacted him.

He was not surprised to find Bubba seated in front of a CRT. Hardly lifting his eyes from the screen, Bubba waved him into a chair. Michael sat patiently for a few minutes before finally asking, "Should I come back later?"

"No."

"What are you doing?"

Bubba continued to study the screen, flipping through rows and rows of figures. "Did you know Tabb High is paying to receive the latest Wall Street numbers over our modem?"

"No."

"Neither does the administration." Bubba pointed to the screen. "Look at Ford. Yesterday it was ninety-five and three-quarters. Now it's down to ninety-two and a half."

"Did you buy an option on it?"

"No. I've been shying away from options altogether. Too risky with the way Wall Street has been dancing since the bond market choked." He tapped a couple of other numbers, then put his finger to his lips, thoughtful. "But when the market's like this, it's also the best time to make a quick killing."

"Are you in some kind of hurry?"

"Greed always is." He flipped off the screen, relaxed into his personal swivel chair, giving Michael his full attention. "What's up?"

"The usual—nothing. How about you?"

"What can I say? The world revolves around me." He paused, giving Michael a penetrating look. Bubba was no dummy. "You want to talk about something, Mike?"

"Am I that obvious?"

"No, I'm that perceptive. Besides, we've known each other a long time. What's on your mind?"

He reminds me we're old friends. He knows I don't trust him.

Michael did not suspect Bubba of murdering Alice McCoy. He realized, however, that Bubba did not have to be a murderer to be a liar.

Nick had heard groans coming from the locked bedroom next to the room where they had found Alice. Cries of distress, Nick had thought, perhaps mistaking what had actually been cries of ecstasy.

"All right, I did want to talk to you about something."

"Shoot."

"Were you having sex with Clair in the bedroom next to the one where Alice died?"

Bubba chuckled. "Wow, now that's a fine question."

Michael smiled. "Were you?"

"What did I tell the police?"

"That you were outside in the front with Clair, stargazing."

"Then the answer must be no."

Michael leaned forward. "Come on, Bubba, it had to be you. It couldn't have been anybody else."

"How does this tie in with what happened to Alice?"

"If I knew for a fact you were in there with Clair, it would allow me to cross that room out of the whole equation."

"Are you still talking to the police?"

"The police think it was a suicide," Michael said. "I keep in contact with the detective that was in charge of the case. Why?"

"Just wondering."

"I'm not going to go to them with this information if that's what you're worried about."

"I wasn't in the bedroom. I would tell you if I was. Why don't you believe me?"

Michael knew from experience what a phenomenal liar Bubba was. Yet he didn't understand why Bubba would lie to him now. Surely he couldn't be trying to protect Clair's reputation, not after bragging about how many condoms he had gone through with her. On the other hand, the question remained—who could it have been?

Could Bubba have been in the room with Clair and Alice?

Michael sat back in his seat. "I hope Clair enjoyed the astronomy lesson. Did you show her the Little Dipper?"

Bubba grinned. "Hey, that sounds like a personal insult. But I'll forgive you this time. How's the telescope? Discovered any comets?"

No one could change a subject as smoothly as Bubba. Michael decided he would wait and broach the topic later. "I'm still looking," he said. "It's a big sky." He had made a vow to himself not to discuss his find with anyone until it was definite. He nodded to the computer screen. "I need a favor."

"What?"

"Use those codes you swiped from Miss Fenway and call up the files on that Randy guy who's been hassling Nick to buy drugs."

"On Randy Meisser?"

"Is that his name?"

"Yeah. I already have. He's a narc."

"Are you sure?"

"I can't be absolutely sure, but he came out of nowhere. He has no transcripts. He has no home address. I think he was planted here by the police. They're doing that these days."

"Why do you think he went after Nick?"

"Because he's black."

"What did you do with the cocaine you got out of Nick's locker?"

"Spiked a Pepsi with it and gave it to Randy."

Michael laughed. "Did he drink it?"

"Yeah. He was bouncing off the walls in creative writing. The teacher had to send him down to the office." Bubba yawned. "I'll spread the word about him. He won't last."

Michael thought of Polly and the permission form. "I'd like you to do me another favor. I want a look at the report on Alice's autopsy. I'm having trouble going through official channels. I was wondering if you could tap into the police files and—"

"Forget it," Bubba interrupted.

"Why?"

"The police department deals with highly sensitive information. It's not like the school district. They have experts protect those files. I won't be able to touch them."

Michael had suspected that would be the case. "The coroner who did the autopsy isn't a full-time employee of the county, but a consultant. His name is Dr. Gin Kawati. I checked around at lunch. He has an office downtown." Michael pulled a slip of paper from his pocket, gave it to Bubba. "That's his business address. You can see he belongs to the ARC Medical Group. They're fairly large. They must be computerized."

Bubba fingered the slip. "Even if I'm able to break into the group's files, who's to say the good doctor will have a copy of a report he did for the city in with his private records?"

"There's no way of telling without looking. Can you do it?"

"It all depends on how their system's set up. It may be that I'd have to go down there at night and use one of their terminals."

"You mean break into the office?"

"Yeah. Or I might be able to do it from here." Bubba set the paper aside. "I'll look into it."

"I really appreciate it." Michael shifted uncomfortably. "I suppose you think I'm nuts for keeping up the investigation?"

Bubba turned away, snapping his screen back on. "I understand how much she meant to you, Mike. You don't have to explain anything to me."

"Thanks."

The door burst open. It was Clair Hilrey. Michael got to his feet, went to congratulate her on her nomination to the homecoming court. The words caught in his throat. Her usually bright blue eyes were bloodshot, and she hadn't been out drinking and celebrating. She had been crying. She smiled politely when she saw him, though, wiping a hand across her cheek. "Hi, Mike. Am I interrupting something?"

Bubba had stood up, too, and knocked over his chair doing so. Bubba jumped for a girl about as often as he went to Sunday Mass. Michael took the hint. "I was just leaving," he said.

"He was just leaving," Bubba repeated, catching Clair's eye. She lowered her head. Michael hurried toward the door.

"I'll leave you two alone," he said.

Obviously he wasn't the only one with a lot on his mind.

CHAPTER NINE

Polly hadn't lied to Michael—she really had been on her way out when he called. She had to go to the market for groceries, and to the family clinic for contraceptives. If Russ's sexual appetite matched his appetite at the kitchen table, she figured she had better be prepared. All day he had done nothing but watch TV and eat. Her aunt didn't know he was in the house, and since she never left her bedroom, Polly saw no reason for her ever to know. Polly had told Russ to keep his voice down when they talked.

But after speaking to Michael, Polly couldn't find her keys. They weren't where she always left them, on the counter beside the microwave. She was searching in the drawers when Tony Foulton, the architectural engineer at her construction company, called. He had some concerns about the float he was building for the dance.

"As I told you last week, Polly, this is a little out of my line. I think Sara would have been better off hiring a company that specializes in floats."

"I told her the exact same thing. But she says the school can't afford it. How's it coming along?"

"The platform itself is no problem; it's the fact we're building it on top of a pickup truck that bothers me. How far did you say it has to be driven?"

"Only a hundred yards. We can have it towed to the school."

Tony considered. "Would it be possible to rent a real float carrier?"

"How much would it cost?"

"They're scarce this time of year with all the holiday parades, but I could check around town. Less than a thousand dollars."

"A thousand dollars is a lot of money."

"I don't think it would be that much."

"But haven't you already begun construction?"

"We're about half done with it, yes. But it wouldn't take long to pull it down."

Polly knew what her carpenters charged per hour. This was turning out to be expensive. Sara had a lot of nerve putting her people through all this. "But why? It's not going to cave in if someone stands on it, is it?"

"No, it won't do that. But as I said before, it lacks stability." He paused. "As an engineer, I would feel better if we didn't use the truck."

"Are you going to be in tomorrow, Tony?"

"Yes. I usually work till noon on Saturday."

"I'll come by about ten and look at it. Oh, how's Philip?"

Philip Bart was a foreman who'd been with the company since her father had founded it fifteen years earlier. Recently McCoy Construction had won a big contract in the mountains near Big Bear Lake for a two-hundred-room hotel. Prior to laying the foundation, a hard vein of granite had to be removed from the soil using dynamite. Somehow, in the middle of one of the blasts, Philip had been struck on the head by a flying rock. He'd gone into a coma and the initial prognosis had been poor. Fortunately, in the last couple of days, he had regained consciousness.

"Much better," Tony said, his voice warming. "He's sitting up in bed and eating solid food. He told me to thank you for the check you sent his family."

"It was the least I could do. I'm glad he's going to

be all right. Give him my best. But Tony, next time, have everyone stand back a little further, OK?''

He laughed. "I'll see you tomorrow, Polly."

Russ came in the kitchen as she set down the phone. He had not shaved. He looked very masculine. When he had arrived the night before in the rain, he had a suitcase outside in his truck. Now he had on running shorts, shoes and socks, and nothing else. "Where are you going?" she asked.

"I have to run," he said, sitting down and checking his laces.

"Why? I thought cross-country was over?"

"I run year round."

"Where are you going to go?"

"Wherever my feet take me."

"You won't tell me?"

He glanced up. "I don't know where I'm going, Polly."

"But it might rain on you. It rained yesterday."

He stood, stretching toward the ceiling, then reaching for his toes, his powerful back muscles swelling around his shoulder blades. "The rain and I are old friends." Straightening, he headed for the door. "I'll catch you later."

"Wait! I have to talk to you about something."

He stopped, his hand on the knob. "What?"

"Jessica called a few minutes ago. She told me how Sara locked you in the freezer. I never knew she hated you that much. God, it must have been awful for you. I knew last night something was wrong when I saw how red and sore your hands were."

"Yeah, well, it was probably my fault." He nodded. "See ya."

She watched him go. He sure was cool, maybe too cool. He let people walk all over him. She used to have that problem. She hadn't told Jessica where Russ slept last night. She respected his privacy, and hadn't wanted to brag.

Polly never did find her keys, and had to fetch a spare set from her bedroom. Backing out of the garage into the driveway, she rolled down the window, feeling a chill in the air. It had been her practice last winter to always keep an extra sweater in the trunk. Putting her Mercedes in Park, she jumped out to check and see if it was still there.

She found the sweater, but that was all she found. It wasn't until she was back in her car and heading down the road that she realized the ax she had taken from Russ the first week of school—and which she had been meaning to give back to him ever since—was no longer in her trunk. She had no idea what could have happened to it.

She screwed up by going to the market first. She bought all kinds of frozen goods and milk and stuff and then realized it would have to sit in the car while she was in the family clinic. It was really a question of priorities, she thought, after deciding not to go home before visiting the clinic: the welfare of her body over the welfare of a few lousy frozen carrots. Obviously, if she was going to have sex like a mature woman, she was going to have to act like one and take the precautions necessary to keep from becoming pregnant.

Walking up the steps to the clinic, Polly congratulated herself for coming here instead of making an appointment with her personal physician. Dr. Kline had known her since she was a child. He was old and conservative and would have asked her lots of nosy questions. Besides, it was more fun this way. She might run into someone she knew.

Polly did precisely that. But first she had a hard time making the nurse—Polly assumed she was a nurse, she was dressed in white—understand what she wanted.

They weren't speaking the same language. Sure, she had read about condoms and diaphragms in women's magazines, but all the articles had been written with the assumption you knew what those things were. Polly wasn't even sure which ones the boys wore. She finally told the nurse she wanted a birth-control method that wasn't too gross. The nurse smiled and told her to have a seat. The doctor would see her in a few minutes.

The waiting room was crowded—thirty people at least, and only three of them were guys. The few minutes had become more than a half hour and Polly was beginning to feel restless when Clair Hilrey suddenly appeared through the inside swinging green door. A nurse was holding on to her elbow; she was having trouble walking. The nurse guided her into a chair directly across from Polly, who had never seen Clair with a hair out of place, much less ready to keel over. Before leaving, the nurse asked if she'd be all right. Clair nodded weakly.

Polly sat and watched Clair for several minutes, all the time wondering what her problem could be. The girl was perspiring heavily, her eyes rolling from side to side. At one point, she even bent over and pressed her head between her knees. Polly was relieved when Clair didn't throw up.

"Are you all right?" Polly asked finally.

Clair took a deep breath, rested her chin in her hand, didn't look up. "Yeah," she mumbled. "I'm waiting for someone."

"But you look sick. Are you sick?"

"No, not now."

"That's good. I didn't go to school today, but Jessica told me the two of you were elected to the homecoming court. That's neat."

Clair sat up. "Huh?"

Polly smiled. "Jessica said—"

"Jessica Hart?"

"Yeah, she's my best friend. Don't you remember me? I'm Polly McCoy."

Clair put a hand to her head, dizzy. "Yeah, Polly, yeah. Of course, I remember you." She glanced toward the exit door. "How are you?"

"Great. Just stopped by to buy some contraceptives. You know Russ Desmond? He's staying at my house. What kind of contraceptives do you use, Clair?"

"I don't."

"You don't?"

"I mean, I don't need any." She got up, staggering slightly. Bubba had appeared in the hallway. "I've got to go, Polly. Take care of yourself."

Bubba took Clair by the arm and helped her across the floor. Clair said something to him about his being late, but they were out the door before Polly could hear his response. Polly didn't know why Jessica didn't like Clair. She seemed a nice enough girl.

CHAPTER TEN

Michael stopped at the gas station where Kats worked on the way home from school. Because of his one-on-one game with Nick and his talk with Bubba, he was late leaving campus. The sun had already begun to set, and he was anxious to shower and get dressed for his date with Jessica. But he had set the investigative ball in motion and felt he had to stop to have a little chat with Kats—just for a minute. If he'd been asked to pick a murderer of Alice, it would have been Kats.

He parked at the full-service isle—something he never did—and got out. Kats appeared from beneath a jacked-up Camaro inside the garage. He had on an oil-stained army-surplus jacket that could have used a rinsing in a tub of gasoline, and a cigarette dangled between his lips. He must have just been in a fight. Michael noticed he was missing a front tooth—and he had been ugly to begin with.

"Hey, Mikey, how come's I never see you anymore? Where you been hanging out?"

"I've been around. What are you up to these days?"

Kats wiped at his greasy black mustache. "Working and going to night school. You know, I'll probably get my diploma when you guys do."

"I didn't know that."

Kats giggled. He might have been high on something. "Yeah, I might be at your graduation! Imagine that!" He lowered his voice. "You wouldn't let me come last year."

"Not me."

"Huh?"

"Nothing." They were the only ones at the station. Michael nodded to his car. "Could you fill it up with unleaded, please?"

Kats paused, eyeing him. "Since when are you too important to pump your own gas, Mikey?"

"Since I started paying for full serve."

Kats glanced at the pump, grinned. "Hey, you're right. You're parked where all the big shots park. Sorry, I didn't see that." He threw away his cigarette and started to unscrew the gas cap. "You mustn't be counting your nickels and dimes anymore. Things going good? They're going good with me. The day I get ahold of that diploma, I'm out of this joint."

"Are you still planning on joining the army?" Michael asked, leaning against the car. He'd opted for full serve, feeling it would give him a psychological advantage while questioning Kats. For the moment, he was the boss.

"You kidding me? Those pussy-foot children?" Kats unhooked the pump. "I'm going to be a marine, or I ain't going to be nothing."

"Have they accepted you already?"

Kats nodded. "Get your schoolin' done and you're in. That's what they told me."

"Was that before or after you got arrested the night Alice McCoy died?"

He had purposely phrased the question to shock Kats. Yet Kats was either too smart to fall for the bait or else too stupid to recognize it. He stuck the gasoline nozzle into the tank, set the grip on the handle to automatic feed. "I don't remember," he said, whipping a rag from his back pocket. "Want your oil checked?"

Michael could have backed off at that point and asked Kats a couple of civil questions about the night of the party. But he decided to push him further. He would get more out of an upset Kats, he decided. The guy had one of those mouths that spilt wider the greater the pressure inside.

"Yeah, you remember," he said. "It was before Alice died. But the way things are now, I bet the marines wouldn't let you hold an empty rifle in basic training." He knew this wasn't true. The marines were looking for a few good men, but weren't above taking a few good killers. Kats didn't know that. He started to warm to the discussion.

"I didn't do nothing," he said, throwing open the hood. He sounded both hurt and angry. "I didn't kill that girl. I wouldn't do that, Mikey. You know me. We go way back. When did I ever kill a girl?"

79

Michael followed him to the front of the car. "It was your gun in her hand. It was your bullets. Your fingerprints were on both. Explain that to me, why don't you?"

"I had it in my car. I don't know how she got ahold of it. I told the police that. They had no right to go to my place and take all my pieces."

"A girl dies, and you're worried about your gun collection?"

"I didn't kill her!"

"Who did?"

"I don't know!"

"What were you doing on the roof porch when the gun went off?"

Kats's pride had been offended. He began to sulk. "I wasn't doing nothing."

"But you were on the second floor. Why did you take so long to get to the bedroom after the gun went off?"

"Why should I talk to you? I thought you were my friend. You're worse than the police." He let the hood slam, turned to walk away. "Get your own gas and get the hell out of here."

Michael grabbed Kats's arm, realizing he might have made a mistake with his hard-nosed tactics. Here he thought he was proceeding logically when deep inside he probably just wanted to find someone to blame. Michael realized he hadn't changed from the day of the funeral, not really. Kats shook loose, jumped back a step. "Lay off!" he snapped.

Michael raised his palms. "All right, you don't know anything. Neither do I. But you can still answer the question."

Kats fumed, debating whether to talk to him. Finally he said, "I didn't go straight to the room. I went into the backyard first."

"What? You jumped off the roof?"

"No, I didn't jump off the roof. I'm not that dumb."

"But why didn't we run into you going up the stairs?"

Kats shook his head impatiently. "I was out on the porch. I thought I saw someone in the backyard."

"Polly was the only one in the backyard."

"I didn't know that. I went to the edge of the roof to see who was there. That's when I saw Polly. She was running into the house."

"Yeah, after the shot," Michael said.

"That's what I'm talking about, after the shot. I saw her run through the back door. I figured someone must be after her. I kept looking for whoever fired the gun. but didn't see them."

"Go on."

"Then I went downstairs, and out into the backyard."

"What did you see?"

"I told you, I didn't see nothing."

"Then what are you talking about?"

"You asked me why it took me so long to get to the room and I've told you. I told the police the same thing and they kept me in jail for a week." Kats was disgusted. "I don't know what's wrong with all you people."

Kats must have still been searching the backyard from his vantage point on the second-story porch when they passed his door in the hall. But the main inconsistency in his explanation was so obvious Michael almost missed it. "Wait a second," he said. "We were downstairs, and we could tell where the shot came from. How come you couldn't?"

"Quit hassling me, would ya?"

"But you're supposed to be an expert when it comes to guns. Christ, you've practically slept with them since you were twelve. How could you make such a mistake?"

Kats paused, and he seemed honestly confused. "I don't know."

Could someone have shot Alice from outside?

It made no sense. The bullet couldn't have passed through the screens on the windows. Certainly, it couldn't have penetrated the walls without tearing out the plaster. And she'd had the gun in her hand. No, Kats was either lying or else he needed his hearing checked. There hadn't been anyone in the backyard except Polly. And even if there had been, even if, say, Clark had been somewhere in the bushes, he couldn't have gotten to Alice. The only way he could have put that bullet in her head was if he had been in that room with her. Now that was a possibility.

He paid Kats for the gas and left.

When Michael got home, his mom told him Jessica had called. She wanted him to call her the moment he came in. His heart sank. Something must have come up. Maybe she'd changed her mind. He hadn't realized how much he had been looking forward to being alone with her.

"Don't be so glum," his mother said when she saw his face. "It might be that she wants you to pick her up a half hour later."

"Did she say anything else?" he asked.

"Nothing about why she wanted you to call. But I talked to her a few minutes. She seems like a nice girl." His mother smiled. "She sounds like she likes you."

He blushed. She knew how to embarrass him when it came to girls—she just had to bring them up. She had been a hippie in the sixties and was still extremely liberal. He had to be the only guy at Tabb High whose own mother thought her son was a prude. "What gave you that idea?" he asked, very interested to know.

"The way she says your name," she said. "I notice she always calls you Michael, not Mike. Also, she went on about how smart you are. Of course, I told her you got all your brains from me."

"Take credit where credit's due." There was no mistaking they were related. They both had the same black hair, the same dark eyebrows and eyes. Neither of them had ever had to worry about their weight, and nature had given them exceptionally clear skin, although Michael occasionally wished—especially during the summer when he burned lobster red on the beach—they weren't so fair.

Their mannerisms, however, were quite different. His mom talked enthusiastically, using her hands a lot, while he normally kept his fingers clasped in most discussions and seldom raised his voice. She was a strong lady, although in the last couple of years or so, Michael had begun to feel her secretarial job—what with the traffic she had to fight commuting and the crap she had to put up with from her boss—had begun to take its toll. She always seemed tired, no matter how much she slept.

Yet today she positively glowed. She had on a light green dress and had curled her hair. Plus there was blood in her cheeks that gave her face a youthful sheen. "What is it?" she asked in response to his stare.

"Have you been exercising? You look—alive."

She laughed. "I'll take that as a compliment. But the only exercise I did today was to carry in the groceries." She nodded at her dress. "Do you like it? Daniel gave it to me. I'll be at his place this weekend. I'm leaving in a few minutes." She added mischievously, "You won't need to spring for a motel on your hot date."

He headed for his room and the phone. "I'd be happy to go to a movie with her."

83

"Mike?"

He paused, saw the sudden seriousness in her face. "What is it?"

"I'd like to talk to you about something."

"Can it wait a minute?"

She hesitated. "Sure. Call Jessie. I'll be here."

He had memorized Jessica's number when she had given it to him the second week of school. Before dialing, he sat on the edge of his bed and took a couple of deep breaths. Then he dived in. She answered quickly. He knew the date was off the instant he heard her voice.

"Hi, can you hold a sec?" she asked.

"Yeah." He listened to his heart pound while she went to another phone. It didn't sound like it was going to break, yet it ached, and suddenly it hit him again, how much he missed Alice. Those hugs she used to give him when she would sneak up on him— He closed his eyes, sat back in the bed, mad at himself. He was reacting like a child. Jessica came back on the line.

"I tried to get you earlier. I talked to your mom."

"Yeah, she told me."

"She's such a cool lady. I hope I didn't give her the impression I'm stupid. I'm not very good at talking to people on the phone that I've never met. I start rambling."

"She liked you."

"Really? That's good." She took a breath. "I suppose you're wondering why I called? Tonight, Michael, it's not good. Something's come up. I have to cancel on you."

"That's OK." *Hey, the sun just blew up. That's OK. I can carry on as a collection of cooked carbon molecules. No problem.*

But, Jessie, I need to see you. I need you.

"I'm free tomorrow," she said. "Would that be all right?"

He couldn't call his bosses and expect them to rearrange his schedule again. "No, I can't. I have to work."

"Can't you get off?"

"I wish I could."

"Oh, no." She sounded distressed. He began to feel a tiny bit better. "If I had known— Dammit. I'm sorry."

"Don't worry about it. Things come up. I understand." Since she wasn't volunteering what this *thing* was, he thought it prudent not to ask. "I heard the announcement at the varsity tree this afternoon. I was happy to hear your name called."

"Oh, you were there? I was looking for you."

When he had seen her talking to Bill Skater, he had decided he would save his congratulations for another time. "I want to wish you luck with the next vote. I think you'd make a wonderful queen."

"Thanks. How about next Friday?"

"We have our first league game then. I'll be playing."

"Then how about next Saturday? We could go out after the SAT test. We could compare answers! Come on, Michael, I'll need someone like you about then to help put my brains back together."

He had to work next Saturday evening as well. Yet that was a week away. He might be able to swing something with the boss's son. "That should be fine, but I'll have to double-check at the store."

"I'm *carving* you into my appointment book for next Saturday," she said. "If you don't show, I'm coming to your store to get you." She giggled. "How come you're always so understanding?"

"Don't be fooled, I have my days." The words were no sooner past his lips than he realized she was one of the few people who knew precisely what he meant. He hadn't intended to bring up the scene in Alice's studio, not again. He said quickly, "I'll let you go, Jessie. See you at school."

She paused. "Take care of yourself, Michael."

Her last remarks had soothed his feelings somewhat. But now he had absolutely nothing to do. He glanced out the window, at the clouds. They were heading west, toward the ocean. He dialed the weather service. They assured him there would be patches of visibility throughout the night in the desert. Good news. He hadn't seen the comet in weeks. If he could find it tonight, he would be able to construct a yardstick with which to plot its course.

Preparing to spend the night in the desert, he forgot all about his mom's asking to speak to him, not until she came into his bedroom. "What are you doing?" she asked.

"Cleaning my Barlow lens." He held the unusually long ocular up to the light, lens paper in his hand, searching for dust particles. "Use this with any eyepiece and you double its power."

"Are you going to the desert tonight? Is the date off?"

When he'd started his comet hunt, she used to wait up for him, worrying. So he'd taken her with him once, and hanging out with him beneath the stars on the wide empty dark sands, she'd come to realize he was safer outside the city than in his own bedroom.

"We're going out next Saturday." He shrugged. "It's cool."

"You're not upset?"

"I'm fine. What did you want to talk about?"

Her eyes never left his, not even to blink. "I'm pregnant."

He set down his lens. He heard himself speak. "And?"

"Daniel doesn't know. I'm going to tell him this weekend."

"And?"

"I don't know what he'll say." She glanced above his desk at a painting of a kindly mother polar bear feeding a bottle to a cute baby penguin. Clark hadn't completely spoiled Alice's artistic fun. It had been one of the last things she had done. His mother wasn't the type who cried easily, but as she looked at the painting he saw that her eyes were moist. "And this time, it doesn't matter what he says."

Michael smiled. "I always wanted a sister."

She laughed. "They're still making brothers, too, you know?"

"It will be a girl." He *knew* it would be.

"Who was that?" Bill Skater asked. Jessica whirled around. She had not heard him coming up the stairs.

"No one," she said. "A friend." She felt sick with guilt. When Bill had asked her out at lunch, she, in all the excitement, completely forgot about her date with Michael. And then later she had figured she could simply see Michael on Saturday night, no harm done. Naturally, being Ms. Free Time, she had conveniently overlooked the fact that he had other responsibilities. She shuddered to imagine what he must think of her. If she'd had any integrity at all, she would've called Bill and canceled the instant she remembered her original commitment.

But you didn't because you're as phony as that phony crown you're hoping to wear in two weeks.

"I thought I heard you say somebody's name," Bill said, stepping into her bedroom. He had on a turtleneck sweater the identical shade of blue as his eyes. And he had brought his body with him. What a stroke of good luck. She could practically *feel* it beneath his clothes, waiting for her. She honestly believed she was going to lose her vaunted virginity tonight.

That's why I forgot my date with Michael.

"Huh?" she asked.

"Were you talking to Michael Olson?"

"Do you know him?"

He nodded. "He's a far-out guy. Did you invite him along?"

"What? No." That was a weird question. She picked up her bag, knowing her glasses were not inside. She would have to listen hard during the movie and try to figure out what was going on that way. She smiled, offering him her arm. "I'm ready. Let's go."

CHAPTER ELEVEN

Aunty's dying, Polly thought. Sitting on the bed beside her, holding her dry, shriveled hand, watching her sunken chest wheeze wearily up and down, Polly wondered when it would be. Next week? Tonight? Now? She hoped it wasn't now. She didn't want to be there when it happened. She had seen enough family die.

"I'll go now and let you sleep," Polly said, moving to leave. Her aunt squeezed her hand, stopping her.

"Are you unhappy, Polly?" her aunt whispered, barely moving her lips. Since the heart attack, it was as if the nerves beneath her already lined face had gone permanently to sleep. Nowadays her expression never changed; it was always old, always waiting for the end, impatient for it even. Only her eyes, the same blue as Alice's, held any life. Whenever Polly entered the room, she felt those eyes on her. Polly, could you do this? Polly, I need that.

"I'm all right," Polly said. "Don't I look all right?"

"No." Her aunt shifted her head on the pillow so that they were face-to-face. Polly felt a momentary wave of nausea and had to lower her eyes. Aunty had lost so much weight, for an instant Polly imagined she was speaking to a skull. Yet, in a way, no matter whom she talked to lately, she felt that way. All that lay between youthful beauty and clean white bone was a thin layer of flesh, she thought, a thread of life. They were all going to die someday, someday soon.

"What's wrong, Polly?" Aunty asked.

"Nothing."

"Are you lonely?"

"Why would I be lonely? I have you to talk to. I talk to you all the time." She glanced at the clock. Twelve forty-five. Russ had been asleep in her bed upstairs since midnight. He had only stayed up for "Star Trek." She was beginning to hate that show. She had told him she had been to the family clinic and he had just grunted. He hadn't asked her why she had gone.

Her aunt tried to smile, her stiff cheeks practically cracking. "You've been very good to me, Polly. You're good to everyone. I remember how you used to watch over Alice." Aunty's eyes rolled toward the ceiling, going slightly out of focus. "Her first day at kindergarten, she didn't want anyone but you to walk to school with her. I remember driving the car slowly behind you. You were holding hands, wearing bright-colored dresses. Yours was yellow, and Alice had on—" She paused, trying to picture it. No matter how the conversation started, Aunty always went off on something that had happened years ago. "It was green. I bought them both in Beverly Hills, at a shop on Wilshire. Of course, you wouldn't remember."

"I remember," Polly said. "Why wouldn't I remember?"

Aunty coughed, raspy and dry. "You were hardly seven years old."

"So? I remember when I was two years old. And, anyway, Alice's dress wasn't green. It was red." She was suddenly angry, restless. If she didn't get out of the room now, she felt, she would never be able to get out. She would be trapped there for ever and ever, feeding Aunty, helping Aunty to the bathroom, wiping the spit from Aunty's pillowcase.

"You must miss her terribly. It must be so hard for you."

Polly leaned over and kissed the old lady, smelling her stale sticky breath. "I have you. I don't need anyone else." She brushed a hair from the woman's forehead, and it stuck to her fingers like a strand of steel wool. "Now get some sleep."

Polly had just sat down on the living-room couch when she heard the sound of the motorcycle roaring up the street. She hurried to the front door.

Clark had parked his bike beneath the tree at the end of the driveway. He waved as he walked up the long front lawn, his leather gloves in his hand, his red hair hanging over the shoulders of his black jacket. Polly glanced back inside the house, up the stairs. Russ sometimes snored. Loud.

She smiled. "Hi, Clark. What a pleasant surprise."

He nodded, stepping past her, putting his gloves in his back pocket. But the instant she closed the door, he whirled around, grabbing her, pressing his mouth hard against hers. She could taste his breath, feel it, clean and cold as the night air. She leaned into him, a warm thrill going through the length of her body. Then his finger dug into her lower back, caressing her roughly. She pushed him away, and his face darkened. For a moment she thought he would explode.

"What's the problem, Polly?"

She let go of him, stepped toward the living room. "You surprised me. I didn't know you were stopping by."

"I told you yesterday I'd come back."

"Oh, yeah." She gestured for him to have a seat on the sofa. "Can I get you something?"

He remained standing in the area between the kitchen and living room, near the stairs. "I want you."

She laughed nervously. "What do you want with me?"

He came toward her. "Let's go up to your bedroom."

"No, I can't."

He took hold of her arms. He was thin as a rail, but strong. "Why not? A few months ago you used to take off your clothes to tease me. You were dying for it." He squeezed tighter, moistening his lips with his tongue. "Tonight, Polly, I think you'll die if you don't get it."

"But that was modeling." She tried to shake loose and couldn't. "You're hurting me!"

He grinned, releasing her. "I'm very sorry." He turned and walked into the living room. There were red marks on her wrists, and she massaged them gently, following him. She hated it when he was like this, but couldn't really say she wanted him to leave. Aunty had been right; since Russ had gone to bed, she had been feeling terribly lonely. Clark went and stood by the sliding-glass door, staring out the back.

"What are you looking at?" she asked, coming up beside him.

"The dark. The past. Can you see it?"

"I don't understand."

"Alice's party. All the beautiful people in the pool."

She wished he wouldn't keep bringing up that night. She had thought about what he had said yesterday, as well as what Michael had said, and had decided they were both wrong. The evidence couldn't lie. Alice must have killed herself. "They weren't all beautiful," she said.

"Jessie, Maria, Clair—those three were here that night, and now they're princesses."

"Maria isn't that good-looking."

"But she's Jessie's friend."

"How did you know that?"

"You told me."

"No, I didn't."

He looked at her, along with his faint reflection— *two Clarks*—in the glass door. "Then how did I know?"

"I don't know."

"You can't remember?" he asked.

"I didn't say that."

He nodded, his eyes going back to the night. "Jessie meets Maria, and now she hardly talks to you anymore. Sara becomes president and she only calls you when she wants money. Isn't that true?"

"No. Jessie's my best friend. She called me tonight."

"Why? To brag to you? She's not your friend. None of them are." He raised his palm, touched the glass, almost touching his reflection. The line between them seemed so thin. "Think about it, Polly. If Jessie and Sara had not talked you into the party, your sister would be alive today."

It was a horrible thought, one she refused to consider for even an instant. But before she could tell him so, Russ bumped the wall with his elbow or leg or something in the upstairs bedroom. Clark turned at the sound. "What was that?" he asked.

"My aunt."

He paused, sniffed the air. "Her. She doesn't smell

92

very pretty." He stepped toward the hall. "Where is she?"

"She's in bed, asleep." Polly went after him. "Please don't disturb her. She's not well."

He ignored her, going to her aunt's bedroom door, peering inside. She tried frantic gestures, tugging on his arm, but he refused to budge. He smiled big and wide. Watching her aunt unconscious and fighting for breath seemed to give him great pleasure. "What would you want if you were that old?" he asked.

"Shh," she whispered. "Nothing. I'd want to die."

"Why?"

"I wouldn't want to be sick like that."

"And ugly?"

"Yeah. Come on, shut the door."

"She's no different from you. Inside, she thinks the same way you would if you were inside her." He nodded toward her aunt. "She wants you to do it."

"Do what?"

"Take a pillow, put it over her ugly face, and hold it there."

"Are you mad? That would be murder."

"It would be a kindness."

"Stop it. She's all I have." Polly began to shake, her eyes watering. She could never do anything to hurt Aunty. She would sooner hurt herself. "I'm closing the door."

He let her. He began to put on his gloves, heading for the front door. She followed on his heels, confused. He always had that effect on her. "I'm going now," he said.

"But you just got here. I thought you wanted— Don't you want to see me?"

He grabbed a handful of her hair, tugged on it gently, then let it go. "I've seen you."

"I meant—"

"See you naked? That would be nice. Maybe next time."

"But what's wrong with tonight?"

"You pushed me away." He opened the door, looked at her a last time, his expression hard. "Push me away again, Polly, and I won't forget it. Not as long as you or your aunt lives."

He strode down the front lawn, jumped on his bike, and drove away. Frustrated, Polly went upstairs, took off all her clothes, and climbed into bed beside Russ. His snoring kept her up most of the night.

Looking at Bill, Jessica would never have thought he went in for foreign films. Yet he had taken her to a French movie, complete with subtitles, and she'd had a terrible time discussing it with him afterward over ice cream and pie. The screen had been a colorful blur, the music loud and deceptive. She'd thought it was a war movie, but the way Bill talked, apparently they'd seen a love story. He probably thought she couldn't read.

All that, however, was behind them. They were at his place, sitting together on the couch, his parents asleep upstairs, the lights down low, the last pause in their conversation stretching to the point where she was thinking, *If he doesn't take me into his arms soon, I'll scream.*

He brushed her shoulder. A start. She felt the warmth of his touch all the way down in her toes. She honestly did. She was one big nerve. "You have a thread," he said, capturing the offensive little thing between his fingers, flipping it onto the floor, and returning his hand to his lap.

"This sweater draws them like a magnet," she said, smiling. She had been smiling all night. Her cheeks were beginning to get tired.

"Magnets only pick up metal, not material."

She laughed. "Very funny."

He frowned. "No, it's true."

She stopped laughing. "Yeah, you're right. My chemistry teacher talked about that in class." Either she didn't appreciate his sense of humor, or else—*it doesn't matter, he's still a babe,* she told herself—he didn't know he had one.

"I never took chemistry," he said.

"You didn't miss much. I have to study all the time. I got a C-minus on my last test." Actually, she had received a B-minus. For maybe the first time in her life, she wasn't worried about coming off as smart.

"You should get Michael Olson to help you. Did you know he wrote the textbook you use?"

The rumor—which Michael had already told her was false—was that he had written the lab manual. "Really? That's amazing."

"He's an amazing guy," Bill said. "When we were in seventh grade and took all those IQ tests, I remember they had to bring out a psychologist to retest him. He kept getting a perfect score."

"I didn't know you knew him that well?" She'd never seen Michael and Bill talking at school.

"We go way back." He looked at her, instead of at the wall he had been admiring for a while now. "How do you know him?"

"We—ah—share a locker."

"But Michael's in my locker hall."

"Yeah. He moved." Her guilt over standing Michael up had hardly begun to abate and talking about him was not helping. She wished Bill would start kissing her and get on with the evening.

He's probably shy. I'll have to make the first move.

She touched the arm of his blue sweater, letting her fingers slide over his biceps. "Do you work out now that football season is over?" she asked.

"No."

"You feel like you do. I mean, you feel strong."

He shifted his legs, recrossing them the other way. Then he scratched the arm she was supposedly stimulating. She took her hand away. It had worked in a movie she had seen. "The season only ended a couple of weeks ago," he said.

"Oh." Somehow, despite a shaky start, Bill had managed to remain the starting quarterback throughout the season. Tabb High had finished next to last in the league. "Are you going out for any other sport this year?" she asked.

"Track."

"That's neat. What are you going to do?"

"I haven't decided yet."

She twisted her body around so that she didn't have to turn her head to look at him, tucking her right leg beneath her left, her right knee pressing against the side of his hamstring. "I had a wonderful time tonight," she said.

"It's late. You must be tired. Would you like a cup of coffee, some tea?"

"No, thanks." She let her right arm rest on the top of the sofa, near the back of his neck. If she put her fingers through his hair, she thought, and he didn't respond, she would feel like a complete fool. "You have beautiful hair," she said.

"How about a Coke?"

"I'm not thirsty, Bill." She contemplated asking him to massage a tight spot in her shoulders, but decided that would be as subtle as asking him to undo his zipper. "That's a beautiful zipper you're wearing," she said.

He glanced down. "My zipper?"

I didn't say that! I cannot believe I said that!

"I mean, your belt, it's nice."

"It's too long for me."

"I thought the longer the better." Talk about Freudian slips. This was getting ridiculous. She leaned toward him, letting her hair hang over his left arm, smiled again. "I'm really glad you asked me out tonight. I've been hoping you would."

"I've been meaning to for a while. I've always thought you were a nice girl."

She giggled. "Oh, I'm not that nice."

"You're not?"

"I'm not exactly the person people think I am," she said, serious now, touching his arm near his wrist, drawing tiny circles with her finger. "Just as I don't think you're the person people think you are."

He sat up straight. "What do you mean?"

"That you're not just some super-great athlete. That you are a real person." As opposed to an *unreal* person? she had to ask herself. "I think the two of us have had to grow up faster than most people our age. I'm not saying that's a bad thing." She tapped his left hand. "It can be a good thing."

Her little speech was not leading him in the direction she planned. He began to grow distinctly uncomfortable. "What are you saying, we've had to grow up faster? Are you talking about what happened at the party?"

The question startled her. "No."

"I don't know what you heard about that night, but none of it's true."

"Wait. None of what's true?"

He stood suddenly, reaching a hand into his pocket. "I don't want to talk about it. I've had a nice time tonight, Jessie, and I don't want to spoil it." He pulled out his keys. "It's time both of us got to bed. Let me give you a ride home."

She didn't even have to fix her bra as she got up. She decided there must be something wrong with his parents' couch.

Bill dropped her off in front of her house. He didn't

walk her to the door, nor did he give her a good-night kiss. When he was gone, she stared at the sky, feeling lonely and confused, and saw a bright red star. For no reason, she wondered what its name was. Had he been beside her, Michael would have been able to tell her.

To the inexperienced eye, the wisp of light in the center of the field of view of Michael's telescope would not have looked significant. Because it was so far from the sun, the comet's frozen nucleus had no tail to set it apart from the star field. It was its position—its changing position relative to the unchanging stars— that had initially caught Michael's attention. In time, it was possible it would develop a halo of gas to further distinguish it in the heavens, but he had no illusions about it sweeping past the sun and lighting up the earth's skies. Very few comets came in that close.

He now had an accurate reading on its position and course. The comet was definitely not listed in any astronomical tables he had access to. If no one else had discovered it in the last few months, it would be *his* comet.

Orion—Olson?

He was really going to have to think of a name for it.

And for my sister.

Michael recapped the telescope and took a stroll around the desert hilltop to warm his hands and feet. Although he could see little of his surroundings in the deep of the night, he sensed the serenity here, the silence. Yet perhaps he had brought a measure of contentment with him. He couldn't stop thinking about the baby. He had been surprised when his mother told him she was already three months along. Her due date was the end of June, a couple of weeks after graduation.

Michael had walked down to the base of the hill and

was hiking back up to get ready to go home when a brilliant shooting star crossed the eastern sky. He was not superstitious, but he automatically made a wish. It was not for the health and happiness of his unborn sister, which would have been the case had he thought about it for a moment. Instead, he found, even in this peaceful place and time, a portion of his mind was still on that night two months ago.

He had wished for the name of Alice's murderer.

A few minutes later he was unscrewing the balancing weight on the telescope's equatorial mount when he noticed how bright Mars was. He had been so preoccupied with comet hunting, he had forgotten it was coming into opposition. Changing his ocular for one of higher power, he focused on the planet. No matter how many times he studied Mars, the richness of its red color always amazed him. No wonder the ancients had thought of it as the god of war.

Of blood.

The one time he had met Clark came back to Michael then, hard and clear. The guy's hair had been a dirty red, his eyes a bright green. He had spoken few words and what he said had not made much sense. Nevertheless, as Michael remembered, his heart began to pound.

"Where are you from?"

"Why?"

"I was just wondering, that's all. Do you go to school around here?"

"No."

"Where do you go?"

"The other side of town . . . Our team's as lousy as yours. But in our stadium, you can always lean your head back and look at the trees in the sky."

Trees in the sky. What could it mean? Michael didn't know, not yet.

CHAPTER
TWELVE

Holden High's gymnasium was older than Tabb's—pre–World War II. It desperately needed an overhaul. The lights flickered, the bleachers had begun to splinter, and the court had so many dead spots it actually seemed allergic to bouncing balls. Crouched in the corner beside the water fountain—exactly one week after her Friday-night date with Bill—her Nikon camera in hand, trying to get a picture of Nick as he leaped to rebound a missed shot, Jessica wondered if a major earthquake might not be the ideal solution for the building's many problems.

"The lighting in here makes everybody look a pasty yellow," she complained to Sara. "Even Nick."

"What difference does it make?" Sara asked. "They're all going to be completely out of focus. Where're your glasses?"

Nick passed the ball to The Rock, who walked with it. Holden High took the ball out of bounds, going the other way. Jessica set down her camera, glanced at the scoreboard. Tabb 30, Holden 36. One minute and twenty seconds until halftime.

"I can't wear them now," Jessica hissed. "Half the school's here."

"They're watching the game, not you."

Jessica eyed the cheerleaders, bouncing and twirling in front of the stands. All except Clair, who was standing by the microphone leading the cheers. "A lot of them are watching Clair," she grumbled.

"And here I thought you were sacrificing your night

out to take pictures for the school annual," Sara said. "You're only worried about getting equal time."

"Well, it's not fair. She gets to wear that miniskirt and flash her goods in front of everyone all night. The election's less than a week away— Wow!" Nick made another spectacular defensive rebound, tossing the ball off to one of Tabb's guards. Jessica positioned her camera to catch the breakaway lay-up. She got her shot. Unfortunately, the guard missed his. Holden rebounded and went back on the offensive.

"That guy's missed everything he's put up tonight," Jessica said. "I don't understand why the coach doesn't put Michael back in." During the first quarter, when Michael had played, she'd used up a whole roll of film on him. It was her intention to plaster him throughout the yearbook.

"That's Coach Sellers," Sara said. "He was the coach at Mesa, remember? I hear he used to coach boxing in a prison until the inmates beat the hell out of him one day."

Jessica needed a fresh roll of film, but decided to let the half play itself out. In the final minute, Holden scored twice more, leaving Tabb ten down. Jessica waved to Michael as the team headed for the locker room. His head down, obviously disgusted, he didn't wave back.

"He's going to hear about it if he hasn't already," Sara said as they walked toward the steps that led to the stands. The air was hot and humid. People poured off the bleachers, heading for the entrance and the refreshment stand.

"He didn't wave 'cause he didn't see me," Jessica said.

"But Bubba will tell him."

"And how will Bubba know I was out with Bill?"

Sara shook her head. "Bubba knows everything."

"Has he taken care of your bills?"

Anger entered Sara's voice. "He's put them off. We'll have food and music, but when homecoming's all over, we're still going to have to pay for it. I swear to God, I think he's already lost the money I gave him."

"You've got to give him a chance."

"Believe me, sister, I'm giving him more of a chance than you can imagine."

"What?"

"Never mind. When's the SAT tomorrow?"

Jessica groaned, feeling the butterflies growing. "It starts at nine."

"That's how it was for us."

Sara had taken the test two months before. She had not told Jessica her score. She was waiting, she said, to hear Jessica's score first. But Jessica had the impression Sara had done fairly well.

"Is Bill here?" Sara asked.

"I haven't seen him." Bill had avoided her all week at school. She wouldn't have felt so bad if it had been because he was feeling guilty for having taken advantage of her. She worried that she had come on too strong. "Is Russ?" she asked.

"No. And don't ask me where he is, I don't know." Jessica snickered. "Doesn't Bubba know?"

Sara stopped in midstep. "I'll go ask him."

While Sara went searching for Tabb's sole omniscient resident, Jessica rejoined Polly and Maria in the stands. The three of them had come together. But one of the reasons Jessica had gone picture hunting—and Sara, damn her, *had* hit upon another of the reasons— was because Polly had insisted they sit in the middle of the second row, which was precisely three feet away from where Clair Hilrey and her amazing band of cheerleaders sat between cheers. Jessica liked to keep an eye on the competition, but she wasn't crazy about smelling the brand of shampoo Clair used.

At the moment, however, Clair wasn't around. Jessica plopped down between Maria and Polly. "Enjoying the game?" she asked.

Polly nodded serenely. "I love it. It's not like football. You can always see where the ball is."

Jessica turned to Maria, who was fanning herself with her notebook. Maria had brought her homework to the game. Jessica thought that was why Maria was getting an A in chemistry while she was only getting a B. On the other hand, Maria had not known Nick was playing, and it looked now as though she hadn't been reviewing the methyl ethyl ethers section tonight.

"What do you think of Nick?" Jessica asked.

Maria appeared awed and sad—a strange combination. "He's very good. They should let him shoot the ball more."

"Michael passed it to him practically every trip down the floor." Jessica glanced in the direction the team had exited. An idea struck her. "Maria, you once told me what a Laker fan your father is?"

"He is, yes."

"Next week's game is at home. Bring him."

"My father would never come to a high-school game."

"But you may be crowned queen that night! Both your parents have to come."

Maria was worried. "It wouldn't make any difference."

"Sure it would. When they see what a tremendous athlete he is, they'll forget his color. Look, just think about it, OK?"

Maria nodded, already thoughtful. "I will."

Maria excused herself a few minutes later. She needed some fresh air, she said. The place was awfully stuffy. Jessica amused herself by listening in on the cheerleaders' gossip. Too bad they knew she was listening; they didn't say anything juicy. Clair hadn't returned yet.

Then Polly started to talk.

"I'm glad Clair's feeling better," she said casually.

Jessica paused. She had been unpacking her telephoto lens to use in the second half. "What was wrong with Clair?"

"I don't know, but last Friday she looked pretty sick."

Polly had not been at school last Friday, Jessica thought. "Where did you see her?" she asked carefully.

Polly sipped her Coke, yawned. These days, she lived on sugar and raw carrots. "At the family clinic."

Jessica set down the lens. The cheerleaders, the girls on either side of them—in fact, everyone around them—stopped talking. They were all listening. Jessica knew they were listening and she also knew that if she continued to question Polly she would probably hear things that could hurt Clair, things that could damage Clair's chance of being elected homecoming queen.

Jessica started to speak, but stopped. If Clair had a personal problem, she told herself, it was nobody's business but Clair's. At the same time, Jessica couldn't help remembering how gloomy Clair had appeared last Friday. She'd had something *big* on her mind. And then—what a coincidence—she'd been at the clinic, looking sick.

She had an abortion.

The thought hit Jessica with sharp certainty. She had not a shred of doubt she was right; she had no reason—not even for the sake of curiosity—to question Polly further. She had no excuse for what she did next—except for another idea that struck her with every bit of force as the first.

I am cute. Clair is beautiful. I don't stand a chance against her. I never did.

104

Jessica closed her eyes. "What were the two of you doing at the family clinic?" she asked in a normal tone of voice.

"I was getting birth control."

She opened her eyes. "*You?* For what?"

Polly appeared insulted. "I need it." She added, "Russ is staying at my house, you know."

Sara had gone to ask Bubba where Russ was, Jessica remembered. She silently prayed Bubba didn't know everything. "I see." She had to push herself to continue, although she could practically hear a tiny red devil dancing gleefully on top of her left shoulder. "But what was Clair doing there? You said she looked sick?"

"Yeah," Polly said. "I was waiting to get my contraceptives—so I won't get pregnant when I have sex with Russ Desmond—when Clair came out of the doctor's office. A nurse was holding her up. She looked totally stoned."

No one leaned visibly closer, but if they had stopped talking a moment ago, now they stopped breathing. "Like she had just had an operation?" Jessica asked.

"Yeah!" Polly exclaimed, the light finally dawning. "Hey, do you think Clair got—"

"Wait," Jessica interrupted. "Let's not talk about this now. We'll talk about it later."

What a hypocrite.

That was fine with Polly. Jessica listened as the shell of silence around them began to dissolve, being replaced by a circle of whispers that began to expand outward, growing in strength, in volume, and—so it seemed in Jessica's imagination—in detail. Then she saw Clair coming back, smiling, happy, pretty, ignorant.

The whispers would soon be a wave, a smothering wave.

The poor girl.

Jessica got up in a hurry, shaking, close to being sick. Grabbing her camera equipment, she dashed down the stairs, past Clair, pushing through the crowd until she was out in the cold night, away from the gym and the noise. Along a dark wing of the school, she ran into Sara, alone, leaning against a wall. Sara glanced up wearily, saw who it was, then let her head drop back against the brick.

"The world sucks," Sara said.

"It's true," Jessica said, leaning beside her.

"Bubba says Russ is staying at Polly's house."

"Good old Bubba."

Sara sniffed. "What's your problem?"

Jessica wiped away a bitter tear. Her victory now would be meaningless. "I'm going to be homecoming queen."

Then she realized Clair's unborn child must have belonged to Bill, and she felt ten times worse.

Michael had just figured out the fundamental problem he had with Coach Sellers. The man was totally incompetent. Yet he wasn't a bad person. He had just asked for their input, something Iron Fist Adams would never have done. Sitting on the concrete floor of Holden High's uniform cage with his teammates, halftime almost over, Michael raised his hand and requested permission to speak. The coach nodded.

"I think we need to make serious adjustments if we're going to win this game," Michael said. "As you've already mentioned, we have to block out more to stop their offensive rebounds. But that's only a symptom of our main problem."

"Oh?" Sellers said. Although only in his midforties, he was not a healthy man. He had a terrible case of liver spots on top of his balding scalp, and for some reason, which might have been connected to the slight egg shape of his head, his thick black-rimmed glasses were forever falling off his nose. He also had a tendency to shake whenever they had the ball—a quality that did not inspire confidence. "And what is our main problem?"

"We are not playing like a team," Michael said. "On offense, whoever has the ball only passes off when he can't put up a shot of his own."

"Aren't you exaggerating a bit, Olson?" Sellers asked.

"No. Everybody's trying to show off." Michael pointed at The Rock, who was still red and panting from the first half. The Rock couldn't hit from two feet out, nor could he jump, but with his strength and bulk, he was able to maneuver into excellent rebounding position. "The Rock's a perfect example. In the second quarter, Rock, Nick was open a half-dozen times on the baseline when you had the ball, and you tried to drive through the key."

"I made a few baskets," The Rock protested.

Sellers consulted the stat sheet, nodded. "He's scored seven points so far. That's three more than you, Olson."

"But I didn't play the whole second quarter," Michael said, glancing at Nick, who sat silently in the corner, away from the rest of them, his head down. Nick had already pulled down a dozen rebounds, but had taken only three shots, making all three.

"Are you saying if I let you play more, we'd be a better team?" Sellers asked.

"To tell you the truth," Michael said, "I don't know *why* you took me out so early. But that's beside the point. We're too selfish. We have plenty of plays we can run. Why don't we run them? Why don't we help each other out on defense? We're down by ten points."

"I don't think a ten-point deficit is any reason to despair," Sellers said.

"Yeah," The Rock agreed. "Don't give up the ship, Mike. We'll come back. I'm just getting warmed up."

"That's the spirit," Coach Sellers said, smiling. Apparently that was the end of the discussion. He had them all stand and place their palms on top of one another and shout out some mindless chant. Then they filed out to return to the court. Except for Michael. Coach Sellers asked him to remain behind.

"You're a good kid, Mike," Sellers said when they were alone. The uniform cage stank of sweat. The coach removed his glasses and began to clean them with a handkerchief. "I understand that you're trying to help us."

"I am," Michael said.

The curtness of the reply took the coach somewhat back. "You may be trying, but I don't believe you are succeeding."

"Sir?"

Sellers replaced his glasses on his nose. "Let's be frank with each other. You think I'm a lousy coach, don't you?"

The question caught Michael by surprise. "No, I think you're inexperienced." He added, "That's not quite the same thing."

An uncharacteristic sternness entered Sellers's voice. "But if you don't feel I'm capable of coaching this team, how can you be on it?"

Michael considered a moment. He had mistaken Sellers for a kindly klutz. And here the bastard was threatening to drop him! "I'm the best guard you've got," he said flatly.

Sellers looked down, chuckled. "We like ourselves, don't we?"

Michael's pride flared. "Yes, sir, I do like the way I play. I put the team first. All right, I scored four points in the first quarter. Look how many assists I got. Six.

Except for Nick, I'm the only one on this team who knows the meaning of the word *pass,* or even the word *dribble.*''

"If you are so team-oriented, where were you last week when we had our final practice game?"

"I came to your office and told you I would not be at the game. You said that was fine."

"But you didn't say why you couldn't come?"

"I had personal business to attend to."

"What?"

"It was a private matter."

Sellers shook his head. "I'm afraid that's not good enough. You're a gutsy kid, Mike, I'll grant you that. But you're not a team person. You don't fit in. You're a loner. Basketball's not the most important thing to you right now."

The words struck home with Michael; there was a measure of truth in them. He'd always played basketball for fun, not out of passion. And now the games, along with practice, had become a drag. There really was no reason for him to stick around.

Nick will survive without me.

Still, Sellers had no right to can him. When he was angry, Michael knew how to be nasty. "I played in every game last year on a team that took the league title and went to the CIF semifinals. How did your team do last year, *coach?*''

Mesa High had finished last. Sellers tried to glare at him, but lost his glasses instead. Fumbling for them on the floor, he stuttered, "I-if you think you're going to play in the second half, Olson, you have an-nother thing coming."

Michael laughed. "Thanks, but I won't be in uniform in the second half."

The coach stalked off. Michael changed into his street clothes. He was tying his shoes when Bubba appeared.

"Are you injured?" Bubba asked.

"No. I'm no longer on the team."

Bubba didn't care to know the details. "Sellers is a fool." He sat beside him on the bench. "What kind of mood are you in?"

"I'm mad."

"Seriously?"

"No. What's up?"

"I've got some good news, and I've got some bad news."

"Give me the good news first so I can enjoy it."

"I went down to your coroner's office today. I told them my dad was a doctor who was thinking of computerizing his office. The chick there believed me. She demonstrated their system. She even left me alone for a minute to get me a cup of coffee. I took notes."

"You can get into Dr. Kawati's files?"

"Yes. I can do it from school over the modem. But it'll take a while. I'll probably have to dump the entire medical group's files onto one of our hard discs."

Michael was pleased. He'd asked Polly about the permission form again and had gotten nowhere. "Can we do it tomorrow?"

"Next week will be better for me."

Michael knew not to push Bubba. "All right. Thanks for checking it out. What's the bad news?"

"You won't like it. Girls—they're all sluts."

He groaned inside. "Jessie?"

Bubba nodded, disgusted. "She went out with Bill last Friday. That's why she canceled on you."

Michael tried to keep up a strong front. He didn't know if he succeeded. The situation was familiar, as was the pain. Yet neither was exactly as it had been before. When he was alone with the thought of Jessica, she seemed endlessly charming, always brand-new and different, and perhaps for that reason, he was always unprepared for the heartache she could bring. She could come at him from so many different angles.

Or else stay away.

Bubba excused himself to return to the gym. He'd heard about a rumor that needed tracking down. He didn't say what the rumor was.

Michael had not come on the team bus, but had driven to Holden High in his own car. That was one break, and breaks were in pretty short supply right then.

He was heading for the parking lot when he saw Jessica standing alone in the shadows of a classroom wing. He didn't want to talk to her. He didn't trust what he might say. Yet he did not feel angry with her. If anything, he wanted her more.

Then she saw him. "Michael?"

Trapped. "Hi. Jessie?"

She walked toward him slowly, looking small and frail beneath all her exotic photo equipment. He sure could have used one of those cameras to record his comet on film. But he'd already sent in the finder's application to an observatory.

"How come you're not playing?" she asked.

"Oh, the coach and I—we had a difference of opinion."

"You didn't quit the team, did you?"

"Not exactly."

She sounded upset. "But you won't be playing? That's terrible."

"There are worse things." He glanced around. They were alone. The crowd in the gym sounded miles away. "What are you doing out here all by yourself? You know this isn't the greatest neighborhood in the world."

Her gaze shifted toward the gym. He couldn't be sure in the poor light, but it seemed she had been crying. He hoped to God it hadn't been over Bill

Skater. "I'll be all right." Then she looked at him, her eyes big and dark. "I'm really sorry about last Friday."

"It's no problem."

"I had no right to do that to you. It was totally inconsiderate of me." Her voice was shaky. "Can we still go out tomorrow?"

He smiled. Maybe Bill had left a sour taste in her mouth. "You bet, right after the test." He had to work later that night.

A gust of wind swept by and Jessica pulled her jacket tighter. She gestured north, toward the dark shadow on the horizon. "If it's not too late, and it's a nice day, maybe we could go up to the mountains. What do you think? Michael?"

Holden High was approximately five miles south of the mountains. On a clear day, particularly during the winter when there was snow, the peaks were undoubtedly beautiful. Yet there were other campuses, possibly two or three in Southern California, that must be situated within a mile or two of the mountains. At those schools, the mountains would dominate the scene. And the forest trees . . .

Would seem to stand in the sky.

CHAPTER THIRTEEN

Dashing down the hall of Sanders High School to the SAT examination room with Michael, Jessica spotted a drinking fountain and stopped to pull a prescription bottle out of her purse. Removing a tiny yellow pill and tossing it in her mouth, she leaned over and gulped down a mouthful of water, feeling the pill slide home.

"Should I be seeing this?" Michael asked, perplexed. She laughed nervously.

"It's just a No-Doz. They're mostly caffeine. My dad always keeps a few in this old bottle for when he has to fly to Europe on business."

Michael looked at her closely. "Didn't you sleep?"

"I counted sheep, thousands of noisy sheep." She took hold of his arm. She was glad they would be together in the same room. She seemed to draw strength from him. She needed it. She hadn't slept a minute all night. "Come on, we'll be late."

"Are you sure we're going the right way?" he asked.

"I'm positive."

When they reached the examination room everybody was seated, and the proctor had already begun to explain the test rules. The woman hurried to meet them at the door. Michael presented the letters they had been sent a couple of weeks earlier. The proctor glanced at them, shook her head.

"You're in L-Sixteen," she said. "Go down this hall and take the first right. About a hundred feet and you'll see the door on your left. Hurry, they'll be starting.''

Outside, jogging to the room and feeling properly chastised, Jessica said, "I hope they don't ask for the definition of *positive* on the verbal sections.''

Michael smiled encouragingly. "You'll be fine.''

This proctor wasn't explaining the rules. She had already finished with those, and was about to start the timer when they stumbled through the door. Jessica had only herself to blame for their tardiness. The night before she had made Michael promise he would wait for her in front of Sanders High. Naturally, on her way to Sanders, she had gotten lost. No matter, Michael was true to his word, and was sitting on the front steps when she finally pulled into the school lot. Everyone else had gone off to their respective examination rooms. She couldn't get over how cool he was about the whole thing.

This lady—a prune face if Jessica had ever seen one—was all business. After scolding them for being late, she asked for their letters and identification. Satisfied everything was in order, she led them to a table at the rear, handing them each a test booklet and a computer answer sheet.

"Print your name, address, and booklet number on the side of the answer sheet," the woman said. "Use only our pencils and scratch paper." She nodded to Jessica. "You're going to have to find another place for that bag, miss, besides my tabletop.''

Jessica put it on the floor. Michael sat to her right. There was no one between them, but with the wide spacing, she would have needed a giraffe's neck to cheat off him.

I haven't seen the first question and I'm already thinking about failing.

The proctor walked back to the front. "I didn't know she brought the goddamn tables from home,"

Jessica whispered to Michael. The lady whirled around.

"There's to be absolutely no talking. I thought I made that clear."

"Sorry," Jessica said. Michael laughed softly.

The lady pressed the button on top of the timer. Jessica took off her watch and lay it on the table beside her computer sheet. Six half-hour tests. Just like at home. No sweat. She flipped open the booklet.

Christ.

Her practice books had stated that the first third of each section would be easy, the middle third would be challenging, and the final third would be outright hard. She couldn't believe it when she got stuck on question number one.

1. WORDS : WRITER
   (A) honor : thieves
   (B) mortar : bricklayer
   (C) chalk : teacher
   (D) batter : baker
   (E) laws : policeman

She was supposed to select the lettered pair that expressed a relationship closest to that expressed in the original pair. She quickly eliminated *A*, but then she had to think, which was never easy even when she was wide-awake and relaxed. Words were used by writers. Mortar was used by bricklayers. Teachers used chalk, bakers used batter, policemen used— No, policemen didn't exactly use laws. She eliminated *E*. Now what? Mortar and batter were crucial to bricklayers and bakers, but a teacher could teach without chalk. There went *C*.

Jessica swung back and forth between *B* and *D* before finally deciding on the latter. But she had no sooner blacked out *D* when she erased it in favor of *B*.

Then she remembered a point in the practice books. If you were undecided over two choices, the authors had said, take your first hunch. She erased *B* and darkened *D* again.

She glanced at her watch. She had to answer forty-five questions in thirty minutes. That gave her less than a minute a question, and she had already used up two minutes! She was behind!

I'm not going to make it. Stanford will never accept me.

Paradoxically, her panic brought her a mild sense of relief. She had been worried about freaking, and now that she had done it, she figured she didn't have to worry about it anymore. She plunged forward. The next question was easy, as was the third. Then the fourth had to start off with the word *parsimonious*. She skipped it altogether. Not even Michael could know what that word meant. Their proctor had probably made it up and typed it in out of spite.

In time, Jessica began to settle into a groove. She forgot about the rest of the room, even blocking out the fact that Michael was sitting close. But she could not say this tunnel vision was the result of a high state of concentration. On the contrary, she had settled *too* much. She couldn't stop yawning. Finishing the analogies and starting on the antonyms, she found she was fighting to stay awake. She couldn't wait for the break to take another caffeine pill.

It was good to be out in the fresh air again. The stress had been so thick inside, Michael thought, it had been as bad as a noxious gas. He understood why many kids, like Jessica, took the test seriously. Most name colleges, after all, demanded high SAT scores. But for him, it had been a piece of cake. He wouldn't be surprised if he had a perfect score so far.

"The team got snuffed last night after you left," Bubba said.

"Serves the coach right after what he did," Jessica said.

"How did Nick do?" Michael asked.

The three of them were standing near Sanders High's closed snack bar. Bubba was taking the exam in another room. They had only a minute to talk. They still had two thirty-minute sections to complete.

"When our guys gave him the ball, he put it in the basket," Bubba said. "But that didn't happen much until it was too late."

"Nick will make his mark," Michael said confidently. "I'm surprised to see you here, Bubba. You say you're not going to college. Why are you taking the test?"

"For fun."

Jessica groaned, taking out her bottle of yellow pills and popping a couple with the help of a nearby drinking fountain. "I can think of a lot of other things I'd rather be doing this morning," she said.

"What are those, morning-after pills?" Bubba asked.

"Bubba," Michael said. Jessica didn't appear insulted.

"They're No-Doz," she said.

"Since when does No-Doz require a prescription?" Bubba asked.

"This is just a bottle my dad puts them in," Jessica said.

"Let me see it," Bubba said. Jessica handed it over. Bubba studied the label. "Valium," he muttered. He opened the bottle, held a pill up to the light. "You've got the wrong bottle, sister. These *are* Valium."

Jessica snapped the bottle back. "That's impossible. I asked my mom which bottle to take and she said the one on top of the—" Jessica stopped to stifle a yawn. Then a look of pure panic crossed her face and she spilled the whole bottle of pills into her palm. "Oh, no," she whispered.

Bubba chuckled. "How many of those babies did you take?"

"Three altogether." She swallowed, turning to Michael, her eyes wide with fright. "What am I going to do?"

The hand bell signaling the end of the break rang. "You only took the last two a minute ago," Michael said. "Run to the bathroom. Make yourself throw up."

"Better hurry," Bubba said, enjoying himself. "They dissolve like sugar in water."

Michael took hold of Jessica's elbow. "There's a rest room around the corner. Go on, do it."

"I can't! I can never make myself throw up."

"You just haven't had a good enough reason," Bubba said.

"Shut up," Michael said. "It's easy, Jessie. Stick your finger down your throat. You won't be able to help but gag."

The bell rang again. Jessica began to tremble. "I don't have time," she said anxiously. "We have to get back. I might mess up my blouse."

"And I hear Stanford doesn't stand for messy blouses," Bubba said sympathetically, shaking his head.

"What is the normal dosage for those pills?" Michael asked.

"One," Jessica said miserably, close to tears. "I can't throw up, Michael. Even when I have the stomach flu, I can't."

"You've got to try," Michael said. "You're tired to begin with. If you don't get the drug out of your system, you'll fall asleep before you can finish the test. Go on, there's time. I'll wait for you."

Nodding weakly, she headed for the bathroom. Michael turned on Bubba. "Why are you hassling her at a time like this?" he demanded.

"She stood you up last week to go out with Bill and you're worried about her test score?" Bubba snorted. "Let me tell you something, Mike—and I say this as a friend—forget about Jessica Hart. She's not who you think she is. She doesn't care who she hurts."

"What's that supposed to mean?"

"Never mind. I've got to finish the test. If she passes out, be sure to give her a good-night kiss for me."

Michael didn't understand Bubba's hostility. Jessica's going out with Bill didn't explain it. In Bubba's personal philosophy, all was fair in love. Also, Bubba hurt people left and right, and always rationalized his actions by saying the people in question must have bad karma.

Michael decided to wait outside the test room. He wanted to keep an eye on the proctor should she restart the examination before Jessica returned.

He received a surprise when the lady came into the hallway to speak to him. "Are you the Michael Olson who won the work-study position at Jet Propulsion Laboratory last summer?" she asked.

"Yes, that's me."

She smiled, offered her hand. "I'm Mrs. Sullivan. My son is an engineer at JPL—Gary Sullivan. He spoke very highly of you."

Michael shook her hand. "Gary, yeah, I remember him. He was a neat guy. No matter how busy he was, he always took time to answer my questions. Say hello to him for me."

Mothers always loved him. Too bad he didn't have the same luck with their daughters. The lady promised to give Gary his regards.

Jessica reappeared a few seconds before they started on the next section. She didn't speak, just looked at him, her eyes half closed, and shook her head. He should have checked those blasted pills before she had swallowed them. From the beginning, he had wondered if they were really No-Doz.

They went inside and sat down and started.

If $2X - 3 = 2$, what is the value of $X - .5$?
(A) 2 (B) 2.5 (C) 3 (D) 4.5 (E) 5.5

On this section, they were allowed slightly more than a minute per question. Michael found he could solve most of them in ten seconds. *A* was obviously the answer to the first problem. He didn't even need his scratch paper. When he got to the end of the section, however, and glanced over at Jessica, he saw she had blanketed both sides of both her scratch papers with numbers and equations. He also noticed she had filled in only half the bubbles on her answer sheet. Her beautiful brown hair hung across her face as she bent over the test booklet. But every few seconds her head would jerk up.

She's hanging on by a thread.

The proctor called time. Jessica reached down and pulled a handkerchief from her bag, wiping her eyes.

"Jessie," he whispered. "Hang in there."

"I can't think," she moaned.

"No talking," the lady ordered.

They began again. Reading comprehension. Michael had to force himself to concentrate. The miniature essays from which they were supposed to gather the information necessary to answer the subsequent questions were distinctly uninteresting. Also, he was peeking over at Jessica every few seconds, worried she might suddenly lose consciousness and slump to the floor.

She's not going to get into Stanford with these test scores.

It was a pity she had waited until now to take the SAT. She would not have a chance to retake it in time to make the UC application deadlines. He really felt for her.

And what are you going to do about it?

Much to his surprise, Michael realized a portion of his mind was methodically analyzing the best way to slip her his answers. Of course he'd have to make a list of them on a piece of his scratch paper. The real question was how to get the paper into her hands without the proctor seeing. He did have a point in his favor. The lady obviously thought he was a fine, upstanding young man. Nevertheless, a diversion of sorts was called for, and the simpler the better.

It came to him a moment later. He immediately started to put it into effect. He faked a sneeze.

During the next fifteen minutes, while he polished off reading comprehension, Michael faked a dozen more sneezes. Then, after penciling in the final bubble, and without pausing a moment to recheck his work, he began to copy the answers. Yet he jotted down only those that dealt with the final two sections. This was his way, he knew, of rationalizing that he wasn't really helping her cheat.

What if you get caught? What if she doesn't even want your precious help?

He had an answer to that. At least he would have tried.

Carefully folding his list of answers into a tiny square, he closed his test booklet, collected his other papers, and stood. There were nine minutes left. The proctor had her eyes on him. She was smiling at how clever he was to be the first one done. He began to walk toward the front.

He was half a step past Jessica when he sneezed violently, dropping everything except his tiny square. "Excuse me," he apologized to the room as a whole as he turned and bent down. Jessica hardly seemed to notice his presence. Both her hands were situated on top of the table. He took his tiny square of scratch paper and crammed it between her tennis shoe and sock. Then he glanced up, and—it took her a moment—she glanced down. Their eyes made contact. Knocking on dreamland's door, she still had wit enough left to recognize his offer. She nodded slightly, almost imperceptibly.

When he handed in his stuff, the proctor proudly observed how he hadn't needed any of his scratch paper. Thankfully, she didn't observe that he was a page short.

"It was nice to have it handy, though," he said. "Just in case."

He waited for Jessica in the hallway. She came out with the group, ten minutes later, and immediately pulled him off to the side. Her big brown eyes were drowsy—he imagined that's how they would look if he were to wake up beside her after a night's sleep—and she was obviously wobbly on her feet, but she practically glowed.

"I would kiss you if I wasn't afraid my breath would put you to sleep," she said. "Thanks, Michael. You're my guardian angel."

"Did you have time to put down my answers?" His big chance for a kiss and he had to ask a practical question. She nodded.

"I had to erase a lot of mine, but I had time." She yawned. "How do you think you did? Or we did?"

He laughed. "Pretty good."

She laughed with him.

He didn't want her driving. She said they could still go to the mountains as they had planned, as long as she could crash in his car on the way up. Even though he protested that he should take her home, she insisted an hour nap was all she needed to get back on her feet.

On the way to the parking lot, she excused herself to use the bathroom. Michael had to go himself. He ran into Bubba combing his hair in the rest-room mirror.

"Did she conk out or what?" Bubba asked.

"She did just fine—thanks for your concern."

Bubba chuckled. "Hey, what's a few Valium before a little test? I made it once with a six-and-a-half-foot Las Vegas showgirl after chugging down an entire bottle of Dom Perignon. Talk about a handicap in a precarious situation. She could have broken my back and paralyzed me." He straightened his light orange sports coat. "So what did you think of the SAT?"

"A pushover."

"Really? I had to think on a couple of parts. I probably got the hardest test in the batch."

"I believe you," Michael said.

Bubba was pleased to hear his favorite line turned on him. "I'm serious. I think the difficulty rating varies considerably between the tests."

Michael stopped—stopped dead. "What are you talking about? There's only one test."

"No. Didn't you hear what they said at the start? They use four different tests so you can't cheat off your neighbor."

I'm in a bathroom. This is a good place to be sick.

Michael dashed for the door, leaving Bubba talking to himself in the mirror. He had one hope. They had come in late. Perhaps the proctor had not taken the time to select two different exams.

The lady was sorting the booklets when he entered the room. "Forget something, Mike?" she asked pleasantly, glancing up.

He had to catch his breath. "No, it's not that. I was just wondering— My girlfriend and I, we're going to talk about the test on the drive home, and it would be nice to know if we were talking about the *same* test. If you know what I mean?'' He smiled his good-boy smile that mothers everywhere found irresistible. ''I don't want to change any of my answers.''

She laughed gaily at the mere suggestion of a scholar like him doing such a despicable thing. ''I can check for you, of course. But I'm sure I wouldn't have given you the same series. What's your girlfriend's name?''

''Jessica Hart.''

She flipped through the computer answer sheets, found his first and set it aside, and then picked up Jessica's, placing the two together. ''No, you were code A,'' she said. ''Jessica was a C.'' She smiled. ''Don't worry, you'll know your scores soon enough.''

''How long?''

''Oh, with the district's new computer system, you could receive the results in the mail in about a month.''

''Is there any way of finding out sooner?''

''You could call the test office. They might know the score as early as this coming Friday.''

He thanked her for her time. Outside, he wandered around the campus like someone who had swallowed a whole bottle of Valium, the thought *I should have known* echoing in his brain like a stuck record.

When Jessica finally caught up with him, he was standing in the campus courtyard holding on to a thin leafless tree that felt like a huge number-two marking pencil in his hand. She looked so happy that he debated whether or not to give her the next few days to enjoy it. Unfortunately, he was too devastated to psych himself up for a good lie.

''Where did you go, silly?'' she asked. ''I've been searching all over for you.'' She grinned. ''What's wrong?''

''We have a problem.''

She put her hand to her mouth. ''No.''

He nodded sadly. ''A big problem. Our tests, Jessie, they weren't the same.''

"No, that's impossible. What does that mean?"

He spared her nothing. "It means you got a zero on the last two sections." He coughed dryly. "I'm sorry."

She stared at him for the longest imaginable moment. Then her face crumbled and her eyes clouded over. She began to cry.

This was another date they were never going to go on.

CHAPTER FOURTEEN

On the Thursday before homecoming, Nick Grutler stayed after practice to work on his free throws. In the game with Holden, he had been fouled every other time he'd gone to the basket. The free-throw line, only fifteen feet from the hoop, was well within his range; the problem was, he was supposed to stand relatively still while taking a foul shot, and he had trouble hitting even the backboard when he couldn't move.

Nick put up a hundred practice shots and made half—not bad, but not great, either. He finally decided that when he was sent to the line during the game, he would just pretend he was taking an ordinary jump shot, and not mind what the people in the crowd thought.

Another reason Nick had stayed after practice was because he didn't want to take his shower with the rest of the team. When the coach was around, and they were working on plays, the guys treated him fair enough. But if Sellers was not present and The Rock— or the other two leftovers from the football team,

Jason and Kirk—were in a bad mood, which they generally were, then he got razzed. If only Michael were around, Nick thought. The week before, when Michael had been coming to practice, no one had said so much as boo to him.

Putting away his basketball, Nick briefly wondered if it was all worth it. Here it was four o'clock, and he had to be at the warehouse by five to work an eight-hour shift, and he was already exhausted. Michael had told him he had to take the long view, but that was hard to do when he could barely see where he was going late at night while riding home on his bike. He couldn't see how all this was going to get him into college on a scholarship.

And he had thought being on the team would impress Maria. Yet as far as he knew, Maria didn't even go to basketball games. Even if she did, and he scored a hundred points every night, she wasn't going to talk to him. Why should she risk it? She was afraid he might kill her.

But that doesn't matter. None of that matters.

Maria's own words. They applied to his situation now. He had discovered something last Friday night during the game, the one thing that was giving him the strength to persevere. It had happened four minutes into the first quarter. Michael had passed the ball to him down in low. It had been the first time he had handled the ball on offense. He had two guys on him, and probably shouldn't have put it up. He just did it on impulse, without looking for anyone to pass to. He missed, but managed to get the rebound. Stuffing it home an instant later, hearing the roar of the crowd— roaring for *him*—he felt an intoxicating power flow through his limbs. It was then the realization hit him: he *loved* to play. And it was strange, in the midst of all the hoopla, in a very quiet way, he had felt at home on the court.

He was not going to quit.

Nor was he going to accept the situation lying down. The Rock was sitting on the bench tying his shoes when Nick entered the shower room.

Nick silently laughed when he saw how quick The Rock tried to finish with his shoes, how he put his head down and tried to disappear. It occurred to Nick that, since their first encounter in the weight room, they had never been alone together.

"Hi, Rocky," he said. "Waiting for me?"

The Rock's finger stuck in the lace. He was not so brave when he had no one at his back. "No," he mumbled.

"What?"

"No."

"That's what I thought you said. But I asked twice because, well, you're always asking me the same question twice. It can be annoying, can't it?"

"Yeah."

"What?"

"I said, yeah." The Rock gave up on his shoes, stood, and closed his locker. He started to step by. Nick blocked his way.

"I want to talk to you."

"About what?" He was scared, a bit, but still cocky.

"Sit down and I'll tell you."

The Rock thought about it a moment. Then he sat down. Nick remained standing, propping his foot on the locker at his back so that his knee stuck out close to The Rock's face.

"I never thought," Nick began, "that we would ever work together on anything, so I never cared why you despised me. But now we're on the same team, and I don't want it to be a losing team. I don't think you do, either. What do you say?"

The Rock grunted, uninterested.

"What does that mean?"

"Go to hell, Grutler." The Rock started to stand up. Nick grabbed him by the collar. The Rock's eyes widened. Gently but firmly, Nick sat him back down.

"Now I've put it politely," Nick said, still holding him by the neck of his shirt. "But you're being rude. And that makes me mad. And the last time I got mad at you, I almost killed you. I'm asking you again, are you going to lay off me or am I going to have to finish what I started two months ago?"

Now The Rock was really afraid, and more arrogant than ever. "You would kill me, wouldn't you?"

"I just might."

The Rock sneered. "And you've got the nerve to ask why I hate your guts? Scum like you doesn't give a damn about anybody."

Because The Rock had jumped him twice for absolutely no reason, Nick found his response hard to fathom. He didn't know how to answer. He let go of him and backed off a step. "Are you serious?" he asked finally.

The Rock rubbed at his tender throat, not taking his eyes off Nick now. "You know what I'm talking about," he said bitterly.

"I don't."

"Get off it, Grutler."

"I swear, I don't. Tell me."

"You're a pusher."

Nick couldn't help but laugh. "You think I sell drugs? Man, you are one misinformed slob. I don't even smoke pot. Who told you I'm a pusher?"

The Rock was not impressed with his denial. "I know the neighborhood you come from. I work there as a Big Brother. Before you showed up here, I used to see you at a crack house on a corner. No one had to tell me nothing about you. And none of your lies is going to keep me from wanting to spit in your face."

Nick stopped laughing and went through a five-second period of total confusion. The Rock a Big Brother to black kids? The corner crack house? But then, in a single flash, he understood *everything*. He pointed a finger at The Rock. "You stay here. I'm going to get dressed and then we're going for a drive in your car."

"To where?"

"My old neighborhood."

"Why?" The Rock asked.

"You'll see when we get there."

Nick dressed quickly. It was half past four. It would be dark soon. He would be late to work. If Stanley was at *his* work, however, it would be worth it to clear up this case of mistaken identity.

The Rock had a blue four-wheel-drive truck. Nick gave him directions. Getting on the freeway, they listened to the radio, and hardly spoke. The Rock drove like a goddamn maniac.

They ended up on dumpy narrow streets Nick knew all too well. The sun had said good night. They could wait a long time for the broken streetlights to come on. Nick could feel the darkness inside as well as out. Yet he did so from a rather detached perspective. He had grown up in this neighborhood, but he did not feel as though he had ever belonged in this slum. He didn't know anyone who did.

"Park here," he said, turning off the music. "Under that tree." The Rock did so. Nick glanced back up the street toward the house on the corner. "Is that the place you saw me?"

The Rock twisted his head around, nodded. "There's no use denying it, Grutler."

Nick pulled out his wallet and removed a twenty-dollar bill. He gave it to The Rock. "Go to the house and knock on the door," he said.

The Rock fingered the bill. "What's this for?"

"To keep you from getting knifed." Nick smiled at the alarm on The Rock's face. "Don't worry, they'll be as afraid of you as you are of them. They'll think you're with the cops. They won't want to sell you anything. But ask for Stanley. Say you're an old buddy. Be sure to say Stanley, not Stan. Have the bill out where they can see it."

"What am I supposed to say to this Stanley?"

"Whatever you want, except don't mention my name. You're not afraid, are you?"

The Rock scowled at him, put the keys in his pocket. "You wait here," he said, reaching for the door. He had a hard time getting out. He was shaking.

Nick readjusted the rearview mirror, following The Rock's slow nervous walk toward the house. A stab of guilt touched him. He tried to rationalize that Stanley would not purposely create a messy situation that could not possibly profit him. On the other hand, Stanley might be bored and just looking for something to piss him off.

That moron had better have the sense to know when to run.

The plain white house had two qualities that distinguished it from the others on the block. It had no bushes or trees in the yard, not even grass. And the front door was split in half at the waist. They could open the top and look at you, but you couldn't go barging in. It was so obviously a drug den, Nick didn't know why the police hadn't bombed the place.

Nick suddenly wished The Rock had left him the keys or, better yet, had left the car running. They might want to make a quick getaway. He watched The Rock lumber up the porch. He was fifty yards away at this point, and Nick could see the twenty trembling in his clenched fingers. He was going to say something stupid; it was practically a foregone conclusion. Nick leaned over and pulled the wiring from beneath the dashboard. He had known how to hot-wire a car since he was twelve.

When he had the truck running and looked back up, The Rock was at the door talking to someone. Nick couldn't see who the person inside was, but he appeared to be a young black kid with a shaved head.

Dammit!

The Rock was arguing with the boy, obviously throwing his weight around. The kid disappeared, and The Rock glanced toward the truck and smiled. It was the smile—arrogant, as usual—that pushed the red alarm inside Nick. Cursing himself for trusting the imbecile not to alienate the neighborhood in a minute's time, he jumped into the driver's seat and put the truck in gear.

He had turned the truck around and was approaching the house when he saw a long black arm thrust out and grab The Rock by the throat.

The Rock tried to scream. A strangled whimper was all he got out. Nick remembered how strong Stanley was. The long black arm shook The Rock, pulling him off the ground and closer to the door. Nick floored the gas, then slammed on the brakes, jumping out onto the street in front of the house. He needed something, anything to distract Stanley for a second. Nick couldn't quite see his old enemy, but he didn't have to. The Rock was toppling into the door like prime surfer beef into the maw of a shark.

Nick spotted a Coke bottle in the gutter. The top had been cracked off, and Nick briefly wondered as he scooped it out of the dust if the last person to hold it had used it to keep someone with a knife at bay.

There was a narrow window to the right of the front door. Winding up, Nick let go with a wicked pitch. Glass shattered glass. The long arm snapped back inside. The Rock crashed to the porch floor.

"Get in the truck!" Nick yelled, leaping into the driver's seat again. The Rock had never moved so fast on either the football field or the basketball court. Although starting from flat on his ass, he was diving into the back of the truck even as the tall black dude appeared on the porch. Nick revved first gear, leaving a trail of burnt rubber. One look at Stanley had been enough to remind him why he had gone down on his knees and thanked God the day his dad had moved him to the other side of town.

If I look half as scary as that bastard when I'm mad, no wonder people are afraid of me.

The Rock started banging on the rear windshield so Nick would stop and let him in, but Nick left him in the howling wind all the way home on the freeway. It did his heart good to see The Rock go from shaking with fear to shivering with cold. Besides, he was having a great time driving the truck.

The school parking lot was deserted when Nick finally brought the pickup to a halt, turning off the engine. He half expected The Rock to leap out of the back and start cursing. Instead, the guy got up and opened the truck door for him.

"You drive like a goddamn maniac," The Rock said. "How did you start the truck without the keys?"

"A pusher's trade secret," Nick said, climbing down.

"Oh, that." The Rock turned away. "You've got to admit, he did look a lot like you."

"The only things Stanley and I have in common are that we are both tall and we are both black."

"Then how did you know I was talking about him?"

"Cops have mistaken me for him in the past. White cops. Now, I guess, you're going to tell me we all look alike to you."

"I wasn't going to say that." Finally The Rock was beginning to show signs of shame, faint signs. Sticking his fat hands in his pockets, he shifted uneasily on his feet. "I suppose I owe you an apology."

"Especially if you lost my twenty dollars."

The Rock glanced up, pulled out the money. "I held on to it. He didn't scare me that bad."

Nick chuckled as he accepted the money. "Then do you have a bladder infection or something?"

The Rock started to speak, then quickly removed his hands from his soggy pockets. He had peed his pants. "He was a crazy dude. He could have cut my throat. Why did you send me to the door?"

"I just wanted you to see him. I didn't expect you to make him reach for his switchblade. What did you say to him?"

"I said I was a friend of yours."

Nick groaned. "I told you not to bring me up. You're lucky to be alive."

"Why? What did you do to him?"

Nick sighed. The truth of the matter was, he *had* been irresponsible taking The Rock to that house. Stanley was bad news. It was upsetting to Nick to remember exactly how bad, to remember how Tommy had died. It was weird; they had been such close friends for such a long time and now he hardly ever thought of Tommy. The last time had been . . .

When Alice had died.

No, it had been *before* Alice died, minutes before, when he had gone into that last bedroom on the left. What had been in that room that reminded him of Tommy? The only thing Alice had in common with Tommy was that they'd both died violent deaths.

"It's a long story," Nick said finally. "Can I ask you something?"

The Rock shrugged. "Sure."

"The night of Alice's party—you told the police you came back to the house to thank Mike for saving your eyes. Is that true?"

"No. I came back to kick the crap out of you."

"Why didn't you?" Nick already knew one reason. The Rock had chickened out when he had discovered all his buddies were gone.

"My eyes started to burn again. I didn't totally trust what the doctor at the hospital had said. I thought I might go blind. I jumped in the shower to wash them out some more."

"You really were in the shower when Alice was killed?"

"Yeah. Anyway, I heard she killed herself."

Nick had never been able to understand Michael's conviction that Alice had been murdered. The facts spoke for themselves, and no one had been closer to the facts than Nick. But now, the more he thought of Tommy . . .

There is something connecting those two deaths.

He would have to talk to Michael about the sense of déjà vu he'd had in that dark bedroom. And he'd better tell him the truth about how he hadn't run straightaway to the bedroom—as he had told the police—but had dashed down the stairs first. All of a sudden, Nick had the uneasy feeling these things might be important.

"I heard she killed herself, too," Nick said finally. "But I changed the subject. You were starting to apologize?"

The Rock shifted on his feet again. "I'm sorry. What else can I say? I thought you had come here to mess up everyone's mind. You can see why I was always on your case, can't you?"

"But you jumped me without any proof I was selling drugs?"

"I told you, I thought I saw you at that crack house." He added, somewhat embarrassed, "I did try to get proof."

"It was you who set that narc, Randy Meisser, after me?"

"You know about him?"

Nick nodded, checked his watch. "Hey, I've got to get to work. You give me a ride and I'll think about accepting your apology. I'll have to put my bike in the back."

"It's a deal." The Rock offered his hand. "No hard feelings, Nick?"

Nick hesitated. "Are you really a Big Brother?"

"I am."

"What's your real name?"

"Theodore."

Nick laughed, shook his head. "God help those kids."

CHAPTER FIFTEEN

Sara started her car as she saw Russ jog down Polly's long driveway and turn onto the deserted sidewalk. She let the engine idle for a minute while he headed away from her.

He is living with Polly. I should run him over.

She was cold. She was tired. She had been sitting in her car in the dark for over an hour waiting for Russ to appear, thinking of the way Bubba was brushing her off every time she demanded an update on the money she had given him, fretting over whether the homecoming tent was going to collapse and smother the whole school, and remembering the good old days when she'd had only herself to worry about. She had been a different person then. She had been happy.

No, I wasn't happy. I was bored out of my mind.

Which had been a lot more fun, she decided, than being downright miserable. She flipped on her headlights and put the car in Drive, rolling after Russ.

CIF is in two days, Saturday morning. He won't run far.

Nor, did it seem, was he going to run very fast. She followed him for two miles, out of the housing tract and on to a path that circled the park across the street from the school. He never broke his leisurely jog. He also gave no sign that he knew she was following him. But when he made a sudden U-turn and began to head back toward Polly's house, she momentarily panicked and put her foot on the gas, racing past him. She probably would have kept going if he hadn't waved. Slamming on the brakes, she pulled over to the side of the road and got out. His breath came out white as he walked toward her.

"Have you been following me?" he asked.

"No." She wished more than anything else in the universe that she didn't feel this way when she was with him, that she didn't need him. "Yes," she said. "Aren't you going to say 'Hi, Sara'?"

He wiped the sweat from his face with the arm of his shirt. "Hi, Sara."

"Hi, Russ. How are you?"

"Fine. How are you?"

"I feel like an idiot. How did you know I was following you?"

"I don't go into a coma when I'm running." He came up beside her, gestured to the unlit park, the silent rolling grass hills. "It's late," he said.

"I remember you told me you liked to run late at night."

"Yeah, it's cooler. And you don't have to run into people."

"Not as cool as a freezer, though," she said. He

tried to brush off her remark, but she spoke quickly. "I'm sorry I locked you in there. I didn't mean to. I mean, I meant to, but I didn't know you'd have such a hard time getting out." She reached for her car door. "That's all I wanted to say."

"Where are you going?" he asked, surprised.

"You don't like to run into people." She opened the car door. "That's what you just said."

"I wasn't talking about you. Hey, don't go." He closed the door, touching her hand in the process. "Come on, Sara, let's not fight."

She couldn't look at him, not when he was living with one of her best friends and sending that friend out to buy contraceptives in public clinics. "I just don't want to bother you," she said.

He put his hand on her arm. "You're not bothering me."

"I'm not?"

"No."

She whirled on him, throwing off his hand. "Well, you're bothering me! You got yourself fired. You've stopped coming to school. You've got this big race you've got to win if you're going to do anything with yourself. And you're—"

"I'm just sleeping there, that's all," he interrupted.

"Did I say anything? Did I say a word about you having sex with Polly and the whole school talking about it when they're not talking about Clair's abortion?"

"Clair had an abortion?"

"Yeah, and it wouldn't surprise me if you're the one who got her pregnant!"

He scratched his head, confused. "There you go yelling at me again when I'm trying to be nice to you."

"I'm not yelling at you!" she yelled. Then she stopped. "Why are you trying to be nice to me?"

"I don't know. I guess I like you."

"You don't like me."

He was beginning to get annoyed. "All right, I don't like you."

"I know you don't. Why did you say that you do?"

Russ sighed, sat down on the curb. "Never mind."

She sat beside him, studying his face for a full minute. He looked about as miserable as she felt, but it gave her no satisfaction. A chilly damp layer of air began to creep toward them from the dark park. "You're going to catch cold," she said.

"I don't care."

"I care."

"What do you care about?"

"That you're going to get cold." She hesitated. "And I care about you, you know?"

"No, you don't."

It was her turn to be annoyed. "Are you calling me a liar?"

"No."

"Then what are you doing?"

He rested his head in his hands. "I think I'm beginning to get a headache."

"Oh, swell, thanks a lot. Sorry I had to be born and mess up your evening." She started to get up. He stopped her.

"Would you please quit doing that?"

She brushed off his hand but kept her place beside him on the curb. Her butt was beginning to freeze. "I'm not doing anything. I tell you I care about you and you don't believe me."

"Well, I told you I like you and you don't believe me."

Sara paused. "You're right." Then she smiled. "Do you really like me?"

"No."

She pushed him. "Yes, you do! You're crazy about me. You're just afraid to admit it."

He laughed. "I wouldn't go that far. Stop pushing me!" He grabbed her hands, pinning them together, hard; impressing upon her again how strong he was. Then their eyes met. She didn't think she had ever looked him straight in the eye before. They were dark, intense. They even scared her, a bit. Still holding on to her, he leaned over and kissed her on the lips. She kissed him back.

Oh, my.

He wasn't cold at all. No one had ever kissed her before.

A minute later—or maybe longer, her sense of time went straight to hell the instant they had made contact—he pulled back.

"What's the matter?" she asked, opening her eyes with a start. She couldn't remember closing them. Nor could she remember him releasing her hands and wrapping his arm around her shoulders. Like his mouth, it, too, felt warm.

"Nothing. I can't kiss you all night. You're new at this, aren't you?"

"No. Why do you say that?" She had a rush of anxiety. "Am I a lousy kisser?"

"Fair."

She started to shove him again. But when he started to stop her, she let him. Unfortunately, he didn't pin her hands or kiss her again. He just stared at her, and she found herself blushing.

"What are you thinking?" she asked finally.

"About something you said."

"What?"

"That I'm a drunk," he said.

"I didn't mean—"

"No, you're right." He took back his arm, rested his elbows on his thighs, his head hanging down. Even in the dark, she could see the gooseflesh forming on his legs. She should let him go, or give him a ride home, back to Polly's house. "I've got to quit the beer," he said.

She nodded. "I wish you would. You'd run a lot faster. The race is Saturday, isn't it?"

"Yeah."

He had kissed her, she thought, her next question shouldn't be hard to ask. Yet it was. "Do you want me to come?"

He glanced up. "Do you want to?"

She spoke carefully. "Will I be the only one there?"

He shook his head, serious. "I'm only staying with Polly because I have nowhere else to stay."

"That's not what she says."

"Then she's crazy."

Sara couldn't argue with that. "Yeah, but she's also my friend. And she just lost her sister." The mention of Alice made her pause. She had all these problems, and somehow, they all seemed connected to that night.

When Alice was alive, it was easy to be tough.

Suddenly she was close to crying. It was true, what people said about how when someone close to you died, a part of you also died. Two months ago she would simply have told Bubba to take a hike. She would never have lost the money in the first place. She wiped at her eyes, fighting for control.

"What's wrong?" he asked.

"Nothing. Yeah, I want to come. I'll be there." She shoved him in the side. "You'd better win."

CHAPTER SIXTEEN

The following afternoon, Friday, Jessica left school at lunch to go home. She had called the SAT test office in the morning looking for her scores. When they told her they would have to search for the information, she had asked them to call back and leave the scores on her answering machine. Naturally, she was anxious to check the machine's tape. The big event of the day was over, anyway. Voting for homecoming queen had taken place during fourth period. She had intended to vote for Maria but, at the last minute, had checked the box beside her own name. Clair hadn't been in all week and the gossip going around about her was vicious; nevertheless, Jessica did not want to lose by one vote.

At home, Jessica found both her test score and Clair. She did not, however, notice her rival until after she had run upstairs and listened to the bad news on her answering machine.

"Jessica Hart," a brisk-voiced lady said. "This is Jill Stewart at the test office. Your scores are as follows: Three hundred and seventy on the verbal section, and three hundred and twenty on the math section. If you have any further questions, please feel free to call me back."

Sixteen hundred total was a perfect score. If you got less than four hundred on either the math or verbal section, your counselor usually recommended a community college with a strong tutorial program. Jessica trudged back downstairs and outside and plopped down on the front-porch steps. She thought of all the Stanford yearbooks she had browsed through while growing up. Her father was going to kill her.

"Bad news?" a voice asked. Jessica looked up and stood quickly. Dressed in old, faded blue jeans, and a plain red blouse, not wearing a speck of makeup, Clair strolled up the walkway.

"Clair, you surprised me. How did you know I'd be here?"

"Bubba told me." Clair stopped at a distance of approximately ten feet, gave the house a cursory inspection, then focused on Jessica, her blue eyes cold. "He told me a few things. All about your filthy mouth."

She swallowed. "What?"

"Don't deny it. You started the rumor about me having an abortion."

"That's not true. All I know is what Polly told me."

"Polly nothing. You made her talk. You did it because you're afraid of me. You're afraid I'll beat you out for homecoming queen, and that I'll take Bill away from you." Clair took a big step closer. "But like I told you before, dearie. I can't lose. And as far as Bill is concerned, you can have him. For all the good he'll do you."

Jessica shook her head weakly, as weak as her lies. "I don't know what you're talking about."

Clair drew closer still, pointing a long nail at her face. "When I first met you with Mike, I thought you had class. I thought we could become friends. Now I'm glad I kept my distance. I hope Mike does the same." She flicked her nail at the end of Jessica's nose, scratching it. "You'll get what you deserve, bitch."

Clair turned then, leaving, and Jessica went inside and collapsed on the couch. It was hard to remember when she had felt worse.

"Alice, where are you?" she moaned to the ceiling. Her little friend had always looked up to her, and perhaps because of that, she had always striven to do what she knew was right. Now that Alice was gone it seemed she didn't care who she stepped on.

Oh, I care. But I do it, anyway.

That morning Bill had asked her to the homecoming dance, and she had said yes. Although talk continued to fly about how he had knocked Clair up, he appeared unaffected by it. Indeed, he hadn't even gone to the trouble of denying it, which confused her; she had recently learned from Polly that it had been Bubba, and not Bill, who had picked Clair up at the clinic.

Once upon a time, Bill's asking her to the dance would have meant everything. And she had agreed to go with him because he still had a body that wouldn't quit. But she was no longer infatuated with him. He virtually had no personality, she finally realized. More important, she was interested in someone else.

She was in love with Michael Olson.

When he had told her about the different tests, and in one stroke shattered her lifelong plans, she wanted to die. What she had done instead was sit in the shade of a tree at the back of the Sanders campus. Afraid to leave her in her fragile condition, Michael had sat with her. With the realization that she wasn't going anywhere special after graduation, the Valium had begun to sock it to her. Lying on the grass, Michael sitting quietly at her side, she had wandered in and out of consciousness for what had seemed ages. But each time she had resurfaced, she opened her eyes to find Michael still waiting for her, sometimes writing in a notebook, other times just staring up into the sky. And each time he had looked different to her, as if she were seeing him through different eyes. Each time he had looked more beautiful, more perfect. Each time she had awakened hoping to find his fingers stroking her hair, or catch his eyes fixed on her face.

But he was just being the way he is, kind. I can't expect anything from him.

She kept taking advantage of him. Surely by now he must know why she had stood him up. Bubba knew everything, and Bubba must have told him. Yet he had treated her nicely all week, repeatedly apologizing for giving her the wrong answers on the test, wishing her well on the homecoming-queen vote, apparently oblivious to the self-serving gossip floating around that she had set in motion. He had treated her as Alice always had, as if she were special.

Not for the first time, Jessica wondered what he really thought of her. She would have given almost anything to know.

The mountains owned half the sky. Had the school been any closer to the slopes, it would have had to have been built perpendicular to the ground. Temple High was his best bet and, for that reason, Michael had saved it for the last. Parking in front of the administration building, he climbed out of his car and headed up the steps.

The receptionist-secretary was young and Hawaiian, with braided black hair and a dazzling set of teeth that made Michael think of South Pacific islands and warm green swells. It had been cold the past night and, from the forecast, would be colder still the next night for their outdoor homecoming dance. He hadn't made up his mind whether he'd go or not. All week he had been trying to psych himself up to ask Jessica. With the SAT fiasco, though, he felt the timing would be lousy. On the other hand, she had given no indication she had a date. Bubba hadn't heard anything about Bill having asked her, and that probably meant she needed an escort. Maybe he could give her a call, work the conversation around to the dance, and see what happened.

"Can I help you?" the young lady asked, wheeling her swivel chair back from her typewriter.

"Yes, I'd like to buy a copy of your yearbook." He had learned at the previous two schools he had visited that people would immediately get suspicious if he asked for a list of all the students named Clark. That's confidential information, they would say, and where are you from, and all that jive. All he needed was a picture with a name.

"The due date of ordering yearbooks was last month," she said.

"A copy of last year's yearbook would be fine." He had the lie ready. "You see, I don't actually go here. I'm on the yearbook staff at another school. I'm doing format research for our annual." He spoke sincerely. "I've heard Temple's got one of the best yearbooks in Southern California."

Never underestimate the power of school pride. The lady smiled at the compliment and immediately went looking for a book. When she returned a few minutes later with the annual in hand, and he asked what the charge would be, she said it was a complimentary copy. He thanked her and hurried to his car.

Twenty minutes later, after a thorough search of the senior, junior, and sophomore classes, he slammed the book shut in disgust. There wasn't a single Clark in the whole school, much less one with ugly red hair and green cat eyes. Tossing the yearbook onto the passenger seat, he rolled down the window and stared at the mountains. Far above, on a high-altitude breeze, the matchstick trees swayed in the hard blue sky.

He must have been stoned. He must have been rambling.

Michael had a couple of hours before he had to go

to work. He wasn't sure what to do next. His mom had said she would be getting off work early that day, and he debated swinging by the house to see how she was doing. She had told her boyfriend, Daniel, about the baby, and the man was excited. Yet he hadn't proposed, not yet. He needed to digest the news, he said. Michael could understand that. He was still digesting the idea of having a dad. At least there was no chance of the baby telling him what he could and couldn't do. His mom appeared to be taking everything in stride.

Not making any progress proving Alice had been murdered had frustrated him. He decided to go by the school and check with Bubba on the coroner's files.

When he arrived back at Tabb, sixth period was over and the campus was almost deserted. Crossing the courtyard, he caught a glimpse between the buildings of the huge tent being erected for the dance on the practice basketball courts. It looked like Sara had been talking to a circus.

He didn't enter the computer room from the outside, but through the central utility room that connected all the science classes. Just before opening the door, however, he overheard Bubba talking to Clair. Because it was Bubba, and because Bubba had more power than any teenager had a right to, Michael felt it was his moral responsibility to eavesdrop. He put his ear to the door.

"I can't do it," Bubba was saying. "It'll be too obvious."

"Obvious to who?" Clair demanded.

"Mike for one. He knows what I can do. And he likes Jessie."

"Would he talk?"

"He might. And even though the votes haven't been tabulated, the word around town has you way off the mark. If you suddenly won, it could get ugly."

"For who? You?"

"As a matter of fact, yes."

Clair growled. "You're always bragging about your ability to get anything you want. And here I ask you one tiny favor and you say no. I'm sick of it, Bubba. I tell you, I won't stand on that stage and see her crowned."

"I know."

"You know? Then do something about it!"

"I can't."

There was a long pause. Michael could readily imagine the expression on Clair's face and was glad it was not glaring down on him. "You think of something," she said finally, soft and deadly. "Or *I'll* think of something."

Bubba did not respond, or did not have a chance to. Michael listened as Clair stalked out of the room, slamming the door in the process. He waited a respectable length of time before entering. Bubba glanced up from his terminal.

"Hi, Mike. Did you discover Clark Kent's secret identity?"

Michael shook his head, sat down. "The more I chase this guy, the more I think he must be some kind of superman to disappear the way he has." He nodded toward the screen. Bubba was presently in an administrative file he had no right to be in. It could very well be the file where the votes for the homecoming queen had been stored. "What are you working on?" he asked.

"Nothing important." Bubba turned off the screen, thoughtful. "Going to the dance tomorrow?"

"I'd like to see how Nick does in the game. I don't know, I might hang around afterward. Sara's got the price for the dance down to five bucks."

"I don't know how she does it."

"Still no word on Bill asking Jessie?"

"It just came in. Bill nabbed her this morning after political science. The slut was flattered."

"Don't call her that."

"Sorry. A slip of the tongue."

Michael decided he wasn't going to the dance after all. He couldn't bear the thought of watching them moving hand in hand across the floor. He should have asked her himself! He honestly thought she might have said yes. Even though he had messed her up on the SAT test, she hadn't directed one word of blame at him. She had style.

Even when unconscious.

He remembered sitting beside her while she slept off the effect of the drugs, her shiny brown hair spread over her tucked-in arm, her lips pursed like those of a dreaming child, her long, thick eyelashes flickering slightly as her chest slowly rose and fell. If he hadn't fallen completely in love with her before, he had toppled the final distance that afternoon. He had been tempted to kiss her while she slept.

Then he thought of Alice. He always thought of Alice whenever Jessica appeared to be slipping further from his grasp. It was as if he substituted a fresh pain for one locked in memory, some kind of perverted reflex.

"When are you going to try for the autopsy report?" he asked.

"Tomorrow. But I warn you, it'll take a while to copy all the medical group's files over the school modem, twelve hours minimum. That's going to cost a couple of hundred at least."

"I'll pay it. Can you start it in the morning?"

"For you, Mike, anything."

"Thanks." Michael almost made him promise to leave Jessica as homecoming queen if she had been elected to the position. He couldn't believe she had anything to do with the slanderous gossip going around about Clair. But it wouldn't do to hassle Bubba, he decided, until he had that report in his hand. And he remembered Bubba's words to Clair, that nothing could be done to change the outcome of the vote, and he was reassured.

CHAPTER SEVENTEEN

That night, the night before the dance and the ruin of a princess, Polly returned to her big house to find a message from Tony Foulton on her answering machine and a note from Russ taped to the mirror in her downstairs bathroom. She had stopped at the hospital after school to check on Philip Bart—the foreman who had gotten knocked on the head during the dynamite blast—and was late getting home. Poor Phil, initially he'd made good progress, but he'd lapsed back into a coma the previous night, and now the doctors were saying he wasn't going to make it. Polly had run into his wife in the intensive-care waiting room and the woman had depressed the hell out of her, crying and carrying on.

But everyone's got to die, sooner or later.

Polly got to Tony's message first, playing it while she grabbed a carrot from the refrigerator.

"Polly, this is Tony. Just called to let you know the float will be ready tomorrow morning if you want to swing by the plant for a final inspection before we tow it to the school. I'll be at home this evening if you want to reach me."

Then she discovered the note.

Polly,

I've found a new place to stay. Thanks for the hospitality. I won't forget it.

Russ

A tidal wave of emotion began to rush over Polly, and then, as if the wave had suddenly run into a mountain of granite, there was nothing. She stood holding the note in one hand, the carrot in the other, staring at her reflection in the mirror and thinking about absolutely nothing for an indeterminate length of time. During this time, she wasn't the least bit mad or the least bit depressed. She simply wasn't there. Even when she began to think again, she didn't feel much of anything, except an abrupt, intense hunger.

She blinked at her reflection. She hardly recognized herself. She was much too skinny. No wonder Russ hadn't wanted to have sex with her!

Throwing both the carrot and the note into the toilet and flushing them out of existence, she hurried back to the kitchen. There was a two-pound box of chocolates in the cupboard above the refrigerator that some bleeding soul had given her after Alice's funeral. Love and chocolate, she'd once read, were practically interchangeable from a hormonal point of view.

Polly found the box and began to eat, one candy after another. They were truffles: raspberry, strawberry, mint, all her favorite flavors. She couldn't believe how hungry she was! She finished off the top layer and started on the bottom, checking the time. It was late, but maybe a shop would be open, and she could get another box.

"These are good, these are wonderful," she said out loud to herself. "These are just what the doctor ordered. And a little drink. When you eat candies you have to drink, Polly, or the sugar will make you thirsty. Yes, Mommy, I remember. Where is a glass? Here is a glass. Now let me get you a little drink, Pretty Polly.''

Polly did get down a glass and did grab a can of Pepsi from the cupboard beneath the sink. But then she thought of the paper cups she had told Alice to fetch from her parents' closet the night of the party. She looked down at her can of Pepsi, also thinking of how soda should always be drunk out of a paper cup and not a real glass, because then it tasted like you were at a party. Then you could pretend the party wasn't really over.

Setting down the glass and the box of chocolates, Polly ran up the stairs and dashed to her parents' old bedroom, where Alice had died. She flipped the switch, but of course the light didn't go on because it was still broken. She didn't care. She didn't need it. She just wanted the cups! Those stupid paper cups. And she knew where they were. She remembered exactly where her mommy had put them. At the top of the closet. And here was Mr. Ladder, behind Mr. Door.

Polly had set up the ladder in the dark room beside the closet and was on the third step going on the fourth when the black figure came up at her back and shoved her hard in the rear, sending her toppling toward the hard wooden floor. For an instant, caught completely by surprise, she didn't throw out her hands to brace her fall. Actually, it seemed far longer than an instant; it seemed as if she fell forever, and had all the time in the world to decide how she wanted to hit the floor, which angle would cause her the least harm. For some reason, the fact she had the opportunity to decide made her furious.

In the end she did throw out her hands, her wrists absorbing the brunt—but not all—of the impact. Her right ankle took a nasty bang. Pain shot up her leg and she let out a cry.

"What is this supposed to be?" Clark demanded, towering over her, a shadow, except for the yellow hall light filtering through his messy red hair. In his hands was Russ's note, torn and dripping wet. For a moment, Polly had the horrible idea that Clark had been hiding deep inside the toilet when she had come home, waiting for her beneath the house with the worms and slimy things in the black smelly pipes. Then she realized the carrot and the paper must have gotten tangled together, and not flushed properly. He had never been one to knock. He must have entered through the garage and gone straight to the bathroom, and found the evidence.

"He's just a friend who stayed here a few days," she cried.

"You're a liar. You've been unfaithful to me."

"No!"

"You've been sleeping with him." He crouched down beside her, grabbing her shirt at the neck. "Now I know why you pushed me away last time. You'd already had your fill."

"He's just a friend," she said, weeping. She could feel his breath, cold and damp, on the side of her face. The pain in her ankle was making her nauseated. She feared at any second he would step on it with his hard black boot.

He paused, his fury momentarily frozen on his face, then he appeared to relax a notch. He leaned forward, draping the dripping letter over her face. "Tell me the truth, Polly," he said softly, tightening his grip on her shirt. "And I will set you free."

"I told you." The water spilt over her eyes, around her nose. It stank.

"Don't tell me, and I will break your ankle."

Polly stopped fighting him. He was serious. "I slept with him," she said quietly.

"Honestly?"

"I swear." It was the truth, the literal truth. It didn't matter that Russ had never been awake to begin with.

"I believe you. Do you want me to set you free?"

"Yes."

"Very good." Clark let go of her shirt, lifted the veil from her eyes. "I can forgive anything, except dishonesty," he said, the anger gone from his face.

"I'm sorry," she whimpered, wiping the gook off her face and rubbing her ankle; it felt as if it might already be broken. "I won't do it again."

"I know you won't." He stood, not offering her a hand, and stepped to the east-facing windows. She was surprised to see they were open, the shades up. She thought she had pulled them down. Clark took a breath of the cold air coming through the screens. "Do you know what will happen if you do?" he asked.

"You'll leave me?"

He turned, his face serious. "I can never do that. If I leave you, I die."

Despite her pain, she smiled. "You don't care that much about me, do you?" she asked hopefully.

"That's not what I said."

"What do you mean?"

He nodded, as if she had answered a question and not asked one, turning back toward the outside, pointing a long bony finger at a damaged wooden shingle a few feet beyond the window. "That's what I will do to you," he said.

She lost her smile. "I don't know what you're talking about."

"You see it, don't you?"

"See what? You're not making any sense." Suddenly it wasn't her ankle that was hurting, but her head—a thick pressure was building inside. "Never mind, I said I won't do it again."

He lowered his finger and almost instantly her head

began to feel better. "How is your foot?" he asked in an offhand fashion.

"It's fine," she lied, before remembering what he had said about honesty. "It hurts." Now it was her turn to be angry. "Why did you push me off the ladder?"

"I didn't push you. You slipped." He grinned. "You won't be able to dance tomorrow. You have the perfect excuse." He took a step toward her. "Jessie and Sara will be at the dance, won't they? They'll be on the stage—up there beneath the lights while you'll still be laying here on the floor in the dark. Do you know why that is, Polly?"

"No," she said, defiant. She wished he would help her up, and she wished he wouldn't talk this way. Yet, at the same time, she felt an obligation to listen. Clark had a certain perspective on things that most people didn't have. She supposed that was one of the reasons she liked him.

"It's because of what's in this room," he said, lowering his voice, standing over her again, the windows at his back. "What's *inside* it." He shut his eyes briefly, and it seemed to Polly he was suddenly uneasy; he trembled slightly, and his breathing was heavy. When he opened his eyes again, he was staring, not at her, but at the spot on the floor near the windows where they had found Alice. He added, "What's inside for now. It could escape."

"Clark?"

He dropped his head back and looked at the ceiling, and then stared again at the spot on the floor. Polly couldn't be sure, but it seemed he was mentally drawing a line from high above to far below. "Your aunt's asleep beneath us," he said finally.

"So?"

He tapped the floor with the heel of his right boot. "What's beneath us feels solid. People always think that way. The fools! The ground can drop out from beneath you at any moment, and leave you falling forever. Nothing's real." He nodded toward the floor, and Polly thought she could see the stains in the wood, even though she knew they had been washed away long ago. "Drops of her blood seeped through the floor," he said. "They escaped."

"No."

"Yes. Alice's dead blood. The drops seeped through the wood and dirt, and now one of them has finally landed on your aunt's face, on her lips." He wiped the back of his hand across his nose and glanced down at her. "Do you know what that means?"

She was afraid she might. "She's not going to die!"

"But she is. She's going to smother to death on Alice's blood." He moved toward the door, past her. Desperate, Polly reached out and grabbed his leg.

"No! *You're* going to smother her!"

He regarded her with calm indifference as she clung to his smooth black boot. "It has to be done. Let me go and I can do it now, and it will be over. I'll use a soft pillow."

Holding on to his leg, Polly tried to get up, to put weight on her foot. She screamed in agony when it gave out beneath her. She fell to her knees, her head banging against his knee. Any moment she expected him to shake her off. Yet he continued to stand above her, at ease, watching her crawl at his feet.

"You can't do this to me," she said, weeping. "I'll be alone in this house. There'll be no one to talk to. They'll all be gone. Leave Polly. Who cares about Polly? Please don't do it. I don't mind taking care of her. I really don't, I swear."

"But she won't let you live until she's dead. Besides, she smells." He shook his leg. "Let go, Polly, and I'll set you free of her like I promised."

"No!" she pleaded, tightening her grip, her tears

smearing the leather hide of his pants leg. "No promises! Nothing! You don't have to do anything for me! I can do it myself!"

She hadn't meant to say that.

Clark began to chuckle, soft and steady. Reaching down and undoing her grasp, he helped her to her feet, setting her against a wall where she hobbled on one foot. "All right," he said.

She stopped her crying. "All right, what?"

"All right, it's your show."

She didn't like the sound of that. "No."

He nodded, smiling. "Keep your promise, Polly, or I'll be back to keep it for you."

Then he was gone, down the stairs and out of her sight. It seemed like a long time to her before the front door opened, but then she definitely heard him leaving; his motorcycle starting, its motor fading into the distance.

Bastard. Alice was right about him.

Polly crawled downstairs—moaning the whole way—straight to her aunt's bedroom. With relief bordering on hysteria, she found the lady snoring peacefully, undisturbed by all the commotion, her face clean and old.

Only later did Polly discover the message from Tony Foulton on her answering machine had been replayed.

That night there was a lightning storm, and Polly slept poorly, and had a bad dream that went on until dawn. An ax was chopping somewhere above her bed, cutting holes into the ceiling, narrow splintered holes from which drops of fresh red blood dripped into her open mouth.

CHAPTER EIGHTEEN

A strong wind was blowing off the nearby gray ocean as Sara helped Russ out of his sweats minutes before the start of the Four-A CIF Championship Cross-Country Race. The storm was over, but a few scattered clouds were hanging around, and the grass beneath their feet was still soggy. It would take a few days to dry out before it would qualify as a halfway decent running surface.

They were standing on the high point of the course, a hill located near the center of Hill Park, a place that more than deserved its name. The spot afforded an excellent view of most of the three-mile course. A gold trail of chalk wound near each corner of the park, under trees and along horse paths crowded with spectators. To Sara, scanning the route, it seemed Russ would be running uphill more than downhill. But since the finish line was right next to the starting line, she decided that must be impossible.

"How do you feel?" she asked, folding his sweats and draping them over her left arm.

"You just asked me that," Russ said, spreading his legs and stretching. He had incredible hamstrings, simply incredible.

"What did you say?"

"I feel all right."

"Your back's OK?" she asked.

"Why would my back hurt?"

"The mattress in the guest room is worse than a leaky waterbed," she said. The mere reminder of the fact he was now living at her house—with her parents' reluctant and soon to be revoked consent—made her embryonic ulcer take another big step toward adulthood. She couldn't understand how he could stay so cool. Then again, he hadn't been awake most of the night setting up for the dance.

Where was Jessie when I really needed her?

There was a ton of preparations left to complete.

"My back's OK," he said.

"How about your feet? Never mind, we can't go through your whole body. As long as you feel strong."

"I feel strong."

"That's all I want to know."

Tabb's cross-country coach, and a number of Russ's teammates, came over to wish Russ well. The team as a whole had not qualified for the finals. Russ would be the only one from the school running.

The announcer called out that there were five minutes to the gun. The colorful collection of athletes began to converge on the starting line. Sara followed Russ as he left his teammates and coach behind and made his way through the crowd. Having won his semifinal last week on a different course, Russ had a low number and was given a position at the privileged front of the pack.

"There're so many people to beat," she said, getting depressed.

"There're only three," Russ said. "I know who they are. They know who I am. You'll see them at the finish." He turned, stopping her from following him farther, smiling at her gloom. "You'll see me in front of them."

She chewed on her lip. "I hope so." Poor words to inspire a man going into battle. She could do better. "I mean, I know you'll beat them." She wanted to give him a send-off hug, but was afraid she would accidentally knee him or something stupid like that. She just stood there feeling dumb and nervous while he completed a few last-second stretches. "Well," she said finally, "good luck."

He glanced up as the announcer gave the one-minute warning. "You know what I would like more than anything right now?"

A kiss from sweet Sara.

"What?" she asked.

"A beer."

"Swell," she muttered, turning away in disgust. He stood straight and grabbed her by the shoulders before she could leave. "Wait, Sara. But I'm not going to have one even if I do win. You know what I'm saying?"

"That you don't like beer anymore?" Behind him, beyond the assembled runners, the starter was giving out final instructions. She suddenly had the horrible thought that they would be off without him. "Hey, you better get going."

"I'm saying that you're more important to me."

"That's good, that's great, but they're really getting ready to go," she said, hardly hearing him, shooing him toward the start. Hadn't she done something like this two centuries ago when he had collided with her the first week of school? Why was he comparing her to beer?

"Sara, you're not listening to me," he complained.

"Everybody get ready!" the starter shouted out.

"Russ!" she cried.

He waved his hand indifferently. "That guy always gets everybody set then spends a couple of minutes loading his gun. I have time."

She would just as soon he didn't count on the guy's past habits. "Time for what?" she asked.

Now he was disgusted. "Never mind."

"Well, this really isn't a time to talk. What did you say?"

"Do you want to go to the dance with me tonight?"

Her heart skipped. "Only if you win."

"What if I don't?"

"Then you're out of luck." She leaned over and kissed him quickly on the lips. "Go. Run. Win." She shoved him in the chest. "Now!"

He went, slowly making his way through the runners. But he knew his starters. It was another couple of minutes before the gun finally sounded and the herd stampeded forward. Sara retreated to the spot at the top of the hill. The clouds flew overhead, chased by the wind. She watched as Russ let a quarter of the runners pass him. She was shaking like a leaf.

He warned me he likes to start slow and build momentum.

Nevertheless, it was disconcerting to see so many people in front of him. His buddies on the team had brought a pair of binoculars and they passed them on to her. The mile marker was in the low south corner of the park, close to the choppy sea. Watching through the binoculars, Sara estimated three dozen guys reached it before Russ did. She wished he would begin to make his move soon.

He did, finally, although at first it was almost imperceptible. The midway point was marked by a yellow flag near the entrance to the park. The runners were about half a mile from Sara as they went by it, and this time—she was monopolizing the binoculars, but no one seemed to mind—she counted only two dozen guys in front of Russ.

Faster.

Between the midpoint and the two-mile mark he really began to turn it on. Heading into the last mile, turning back toward the starting line—and the finish line—he had drawn even with the leaders, a pack of three kids. Sara could actually see their expressions in the binoculars. Each one looked determined to win. But she hesitated to check Russ's face, afraid she would find him whistling to himself.

Pounding into the far end of the valley that lay beneath the hill upon which she stood, Russ accelerated sharply, drawing away from the others.

"Go!" she yelled.

Ten yards, fifteen yards, twenty yards—his lead grew almost as if by magic. Sara was beside herself with excitement. She forgot about being ASB president, about homecoming, about being cool. She started to cheer like a maniac.

"Russ!"

Coming up the hill, running right past her, he twisted his head around and looked at her. His breathing was labored and his red brow dripped with sweat. He smiled, anyway.

Then he slipped on the wet grass, and went down.

"Get up!" she screamed, leaping forward to help him. He had only fallen to his knees, and because he had been coming up the steep hill, his speed had not been that great. He was all right. He brushed off her hands and was on his way again before his lead disintegrated altogether.

He won by ten yards. Sara had about ten seconds to savor the victory before learning he had been disqualified. The coach told her while Russ was recovering in the chute.

"What?" she cried. "What did he do wrong? This isn't gymnastics! Since when do they take off points for slipping?"

The coach's disappointment was obvious. "He wasn't disqualified for slipping, but for receiving outside help during the course of the race."

She was aghast. "Outside help? You're not talking about *me?*"

"I'm afraid so, Sara," he said sympathetically.

"But I didn't help him. If anything, I just got in his way. Where's the race director? We have to talk to him."

The coach stopped her. "It will do no good."

"But it wasn't his fault that I helped him!"

"It doesn't matter. Because Russ won by such a narrow margin, he might have lost if you hadn't helped him. Disqualification is therefore automatic." The coach glanced toward Russ, who had begun to catch his breath. He was shaking the hand of the fellow behind him in the chute. "It's a real shame," the coach said. "He ran a brilliant race."

Sara's voice cracked. "Does he know?"

"He knows."

This is not fair. This is not right. This is not happening.

Sara was afraid to go near Russ. The coach was being cool, but Russ's teammates were looking at her and shaking their heads. Russ would probably want to rip her head off. Had the positions been reversed, she would have wanted blood. She didn't know what to do. She wished she could simply leave, but they had come in the same car. She decided to go to the car, anyway. Maybe he would think she had left or forget she existed and get another ride.

To where? He's staying at my house!

She was as furious as she was hurt. Once inside her car, his sweats lying across her lap, she began to pound the steering wheel with her fists. She still couldn't believe how strict they were. You'd think she'd given him an injection of speed or steroids or something! If they'd covered the course with plastic before it rained, he wouldn't have slipped in the first place. It was all their fault. She was going to write a nasty letter to somebody. She was the president of the school. She was going to . . .

"Hey, I need my sweats," Russ said, standing outside the car door. She jumped in her seat, smacking her head on the ceiling. "It's cold out here."

Keeping her eyes fixed on the ground, Sara slowly got out of the car and gave him his sweats. She stared at his feet while he put them on. There was mud on the bottom of his shoes, and no doubt it would mess up her car, but she wasn't going to ask him to scrape it off if he still wanted to ride home with her. She was afraid she was going to start crying.

"Hey, aren't you going to congratulate me?" he asked.

She glanced up and was surprised to discover he looked very much as he had before the start of the race; a little more tired perhaps, and certainly more sweaty, but far from devastated. "But you lost," she mumbled. "I got you disqualified."

He waved away the remark as he had waved away her concerns about the starter. "Everybody knows I won, I just don't get the trophy. Big deal. This way we don't have to wait around for the award ceremony. Come on, let's go to that McDonald's we ate at when we went out that night. I'm starving."

"You're crazy," she said, her voice incredulous.

He frowned. "What's wrong with McDonald's? They use the same hamburger a fancy restaurant does. They just don't charge you an arm and a leg. You know what your problem is, Sara? You don't know how to find a bargain. Take that can of Spam you bought— Hey, what are you laughing at?"

"You!" she burst out. "You idiot!"

He scratched his head, his frown deepening. "If I'm such an idiot, how come I know how to save money using coupons?"

Sara had to catch her breath to speak. Although

from the outside she appeared in much better spirits than a minute ago, she was still upset. "Russ, that's not what I'm talking about. Because of me, you're not the champion. It's not going to go in the records that you won today. College coaches across the country won't know you won. It won't even go down that you placed."

"So?"

"So you probably won't get offered a scholarship."

"Who cares?"

"I care! I care about your future. That you have one. Russ, we're not going to be in high school for the rest of our lives."

He didn't answer right away, but leaned against the car instead, looking out to the sea. The sea gulls were having a great time in the wind, soaring hundreds of feet into the air on powerful updrafts and then diving down at breathtaking speeds to within inches of the choppy water. Russ reached out his arm and hugged her to his side.

"I don't run to win scholarships," he said seriously. "I run because it makes me feel alive. School doesn't do that for me. School isn't where I belong. Sure, I'll graduate and everything, but that's it."

"But don't you want to get ahead?"

"I can get ahead without a fancy diploma." He glanced toward the hill from where she had watched the race. "When I broke away from the pack, I felt something. I felt powerful, like I could do anything." He squeezed her shoulder. "Remember what you said when we were fighting in the store freezer? That I could be in the Olympics? Well, Sara, I think you were right."

She chuckled, not sure what to think, brushing his hair out of his eyes. "You idiot," she repeated quietly. Then she wrinkled her nose. "McDonald's?"

"I like their food. And then, tonight, I'll take you to that dance."

She shook her head. "I'm afraid not, pal."

"Huh?"

"You didn't win."

CHAPTER NINETEEN

Halftime had just begun and Jessica was doing pretty much what she had done the week before at the start of halftime: changing the film in her camera, wondering if all her pictures were out of focus, watching Clair out the corners of her out-of-focus eyes, and listening to Sara complain.

There were, however, a couple of differences. First of all this game was a lot more exciting. It counted in the league standing, and the score was tied. Nick was tearing up the floor: rebounding, blocking shots, slam-dunking the ball. The most amazing thing, though, was he was doing all this with the earnest cooperation of his teammates. The Rock and Nick had been high-fiving it all night. Amazing.

There were also about four times the number of people present. Tabb's gymnasium was far larger than Holden High's, but it was obvious the main reason for the extra numbers was because the dance followed the game. Judging by the clothes of the majority of the crowd, it appeared that practically everyone had come for both events. Like Maria and Clair—and probably Cindy Fosmeyer, wherever she was—Jessica had yet to change into her princess gown. Jessica had had her hair permed and teased, however, and could not believe the abandon with which Clair had led the cheers throughout the first half. Clair did not appear concerned about looking perfect. Indeed, she had seemed quite happy all night.

"You may as well know, dearie, I can't lose."

That worried Jessica.

"Then this idiot with a camera stepped in front of Russ and tripped him," Sara was saying. "Naturally, I grabbed the guy by the arm and pulled him aside. And they called that interference! They disqualified Russ for that! Can you believe it?"

"No," Jessica said, bending over for a drink from the fountain in the corner of the gym. The two of them were down on the floor. The team had left moments ago for the locker room and most of the crowd was heading for the refreshment stand or a breath of air outside. Her date for the dance, Bill Skater, was sitting with his football buddies a couple of rows above where the cheerleaders had performed. Jessica had been searching for Michael all night but hadn't seen him.

"What do you mean?" Sara asked, indignant.

"I don't believe you," Jessica said, finishing her drink and slipping a lens cap over her camera. "What really happened?"

Sara put a hand on her hip, which she often did when her credibility was being questioned. "I bet you think *I* tripped him?"

"Well, you locked him in a freezer once."

"You didn't have to bring that up. That was an accident. And what does it matter how he got disqualified? The fact remains he won the goddamn race and they didn't give him the goddamn trophy."

"Does he care?"

"No."

"Then what's the problem?" Jessica asked.

"There isn't a problem. I'm just making conversation. What a stupid question. The biggest social event of the school year is about to take place and if it bombs it will be totally my fault."

"What about me? I have a shot at the biggest social title of the year, and if I don't win I'll—I'll go out and get bombed."

"You're going to win."

"How do you know? You don't know anything." Jessica glared in the direction of the cheerleaders. "She shouldn't look so goddamn confident." Clair was little more than a blond blur to her at this distance.

"Quit swearing," Sara said.

"Go to hell."

They stared at each other a moment and then laughed. "Bitch of a night," Sara said.

"It's going to get worse. Hey, I've got to check on Maria and her folks."

Sara nodded. "I'll catch you in the dressing room after the game. Remember, HB-twenty-two."

"Good, yeah. Go light the tent on fire."

"Don't tempt me," Sara said.

Crossing the basketball court, her photo equipment stuffed in a bag hanging over her shoulder, Jessica again searched the stands for Michael. She thought he probably wouldn't attend the dance—he had never struck her as the type that went in for big phony get-togethers—but Nick was his friend, he should have come to the game. Maybe if she put on her glasses she'd find him. She didn't just want to talk to him, she wanted to have *a* talk with him. All day long, from the instant she had woken up this morning, a frightening conviction had been growing inside her. She felt she absolutely had to get him alone and confess how she had stood him up, and then tell him how she really felt about him. What made this conviction so frightening—besides the usual reason that she would be risking outright rejection, which was nothing to sneeze at—was that she *knew* if she didn't do it now, she wouldn't be able to do it later. She didn't know how or why she felt this way. She certainly didn't feel lightning was going to strike him or her down. But there was something—something in the air.

What would Alice have wanted?

Alice had known Michael almost a year before her death and had never mentioned him. It still bothered her.

Did Alice feel Michael was too good for me?

That was nonsense. Alice had loved her. And yet, according to Polly, Alice had *worshiped* Michael. Jessica would have given a lot to be able to ask Alice how she really felt.

Bill waved to her as she came up the steps but did not stand or otherwise show any sign that he wanted her to join him amid the herd of jocks. She didn't mind. Besides wanting to speak to Maria, she needed to check on Polly. Poor Polly was limping around like a deer with its foot caught in a bear trap. She had fallen off a ladder the night before, she said. Jessica wished Polly had a date. She was worried how Polly would feel when Russ and Sara danced together.

Maria's parents made a handsome couple. Jessica had been particularly taken by Mrs. Gonzales. The woman had Maria's soft-spoken manner, only to a much greater degree. Jessica wasn't sure how much English she knew. She also resembled her daughter, but was considerably more beautiful, with finer features and wide red lips.

Jessica took a seat on the bleachers between Maria and Polly; Maria's parents were sitting to her far right, speaking quietly to each other. Jessica hadn't told her own parents what tonight was. She didn't want them present if she should lose.

But if I win, I might have the guts to tell Dad about the SAT.

"What do your parents think of Nick now?" Jessica whispered in Maria's ear.

"My dad says he's unstoppable," she whispered back.

"Does that mean he likes him?"

Maria smiled and nodded. "I think so."

"What does your mom say?"

"That he's tall."

"That sounds positive. Ask him to the dance."

Maria looked terrified. "We'll see."

Jessica turned her attention to Polly, who had brought a sketch pad and a number of pencils. This was sort of odd because Polly drew about as well as your average alligator. The pad had belonged to Alice. As far as Jessica could tell, Polly hadn't done anything with it all night. At the moment she was staring off into the distance, her eyes dark.

"Are you all right?" Jessica asked.

Polly blinked and slowly looked at Jessica. "I'm tired. I had a bad night. The lightning." She gestured feebly. "Everything."

The reference to lightning made Jessica pause and remember the days Polly had spent in the hospital after her parents had died. Those had been dark times, almost as dark as when Alice had died. To this day, Jessica occasionally wondered if the doctors hadn't compounded the situation by using electroshock to alleviate Polly's depression.

A lightning bolt across the brain.

Polly wouldn't remember. They knocked you out—so Jessica had read—before they taped on the wires.

"How's your aunt?" Jessica asked.

"Dying."

"Are you sure you're all right? I could give you a ride home?"

"I'm fine, I have my own car. I don't want to go

home, anyway. I don't want to use my ankle as an excuse not to dance."

"What? Surely you're not going to dance on that foot?"

"I don't mind the pain." Polly turned away and added wearily, "It's better than lying on a floor in the dark."

Michael was bent over a CRT with Bubba in the computer room when they heard the cheer in the gym. That day, all day, Bubba had run a pipeline—via a modem—between Dr. Gin Kawati's ARC Medical Group and Tabb High. The end result was a packed hard disc and a ton of files they couldn't directly read.

"The second half must be about to start," Bubba said.

"I don't know if I'll watch it. I'd like to look at that autopsy report tonight."

"Tonight might be asking too much." Bubba pointed to the data on the screen. "These are binary files, not text. Our word processor can't access them."

"We can use the sector editor and read them manually."

"Yeah, but we're talking about forty megabytes of data. There must be sixty or seventy files here. You'll have to load in each file individually, do an 'Alice McCoy' search, delete the file, then load in the next one until you find her. That could take a long time."

"I have time," Michael said.

"If that's how you feel," Bubba said, surrendering his seat in front of the screen. Michael sat down and called up the sector editor while Bubba took down a fresh-from-the-cleaners suit of clothes hanging in the corner of the room. Naturally, it was not an ordinary suit Bubba had selected for the big night. A bright yellow, it came with a green hat. Bubba liked hats. "Will you be coming to the dance?" he asked casually, pulling off the plastic and inspecting the material.

"I doubt it."

"Not even for the crowning?"

Michael glanced at him. "Why don't you just tell me who's going to win?"

Bubba smiled. "I don't know everything, you know." He held out his green tie. "Is this too Irish or what?"

"No one can ever be too Irish. You're changing the subject."

Bubba set aside his suit, spoke seriously. "I knew you were standing outside the room when Clair was complaining to me about Jessie."

"How?"

Bubba shrugged, indicating it wasn't important. "Clair should be homecoming queen. She's prettier than Jessie."

"In your opinion. Anyway, pretty isn't everything. All I'm asking for is a fair vote."

"Why ask now? The name has already been recorded and placed in a sealed envelope. If I'm not mistaken, Mr. Bark has it in his pocket at this exact moment."

"Whose name is inside?"

"You put me on the spot, Mike. Clair did that to me, too."

"Then you did arrange for Clair to win?"

"I didn't say that. What I said was she deserves to win. Jessie resorted to low-level tactics in this campaign."

Bubba wouldn't look at him, and ordinarily Bubba wouldn't mind looking you in the eye while telling you he was sleeping with your girlfriend. "*Did* Clair have an abortion?" Michael asked, remembering how she had come to Bubba the afternoon she had been elected to the court, her eyes red.

"A vile and vicious rumor started by the vile and vicious Jessica Hart. No, she didn't."

"Was it yours?"

Bubba snapped his head up. "No." Then he relaxed, adding with a chuckle, "You know how careful I am about such matters."

"Yeah, you're careful," Michael muttered, confused at Bubba's behavior. He wasn't simply being evasive—Bubba never actually told the precise truth, except when it benefited him to do so, which was rarely—he was uneasy. And ordinarily he would not have been worried about having knocked Clair up any more than he would have been concerned about having knocked Jessica down.

Someone banged at the door. "Yeah," Bubba called out.

Kats walked in, surprising Michael. Kats had changed from his usual crusty jeans and oily army-fatigue jacket into a pair of black slacks, a white shirt, and a red tie. It was remarkable—he looked greasier than ever.

"What are you doing here?" Michael asked.

Kats grinned. "I'm the man tonight. I'm taking care of the princesses."

"Kats is driving the float into the tent before the crowning," Bubba explained.

"Why did Sara pick you?" Michael asked.

Kats scowled. "Is there something wrong with me, Mikey?"

Obviously Kats was still mad at him from the last time they had talked at the gas station. "Kats is a great driver," Bubba said. "Sara chose him as a favor to me."

"What favor does Sara owe you?" Michael asked.

Bubba brightened at the question and picked up his

yellow suit and green hat. "Honestly, Mike, you know I'm a gentleman."

Bubba and Kats left together, leaving Michael's last question unanswered. Michael turned back to the computer screen. Hopefully, somewhere in all this data, was the answer to more important questions.

Michael read in a file, set the computer to search for the McCoy name, sat back, and waited. He wished he knew how the files were organized, which ones he should concentrate on. He heard another loud cheer come from the gym and checked his watch. The second half was definitely under way. He had been pleased to see Nick doing so well, particularly with the cooperation of The Rock. Michael had not had a chance to talk to Nick the last couple of days; he didn't know what had changed between the two. But it had clearly been a change for the better. At least somebody was making progress somewhere.

I can't complain.

His mother's boyfriend had finally come to a decision. He had proposed marriage, and his mom had accepted. Michael had to admit she had never seemed happier.

I'm going to have a father. I have a sister on the way, a comet in the sky that belongs to me. What else can I expect?

Nothing. And yet, he was lonely, desperately lonely. Jessica—crazy as it sounded even to him—he sometimes believed he needed her simply to go on living. And he hadn't felt that way even in the depths of his despair over Alice. He kept remembering sitting beside her while she slept under the tree after the SAT. He should have lain down and slept beside her. Then maybe he could have met her in a dream and told her all the things he couldn't tell her when he was awake.

Go forward, I will follow.

That was a dream he hadn't had in a while.

Alice wasn't in the first file. She wasn't in the second or the third. He began to worry that he would go through all the files and discover Dr. Kawati hadn't bothered to put the autopsy reports he did for the county into his business computer.

The fourth file turned out to be huge. Michael prowled the room while the name search went on and on, listening to the sporadic roar of the gymnasium crowd, thinking of how cute Jessica had looked during the first half crouched at the end of the court, her camera balanced on her knee, her long brown hair hanging loose and wonderful. He glanced again at the computer screen, the endless succession of numbers and text creeping by, and decided a quick stop inside the gym wouldn't make any difference.

He felt the tension the moment he entered the building. A glance at the scoreboard said it all: Tabb 56, Westminister 57. Seven seconds left. Tabb had the ball. Nick had just called time out, and the team was huddling around Coach Sellers. The man would probably advise them to dribble out the clock.

Everybody was standing. Everybody except Jessica. Michael spotted her kneeling alone on the court floor behind Tabb's basket, doing a trial focus with her camera. He wondered if he should accidentally try to bump into her when the game was over. But he could imagine Bill coming up if he tried to talk to her, taking her hand, and leading her away to the dance.

I'll just see who wins, and then go back to the room.

Sitting down, Nick grabbed a towel and wiped the sweat from his brow, trying to block out the noise of the cheerleaders at his back while listening to what the coach was saying. He was running on adrenaline, hyped up. He had played hard all night, but with each passing minute, he felt himself growing stronger. He was ready to take the last shot.

"Go Tabb! Go team! Take the ball and stuff it mean!"

To his disappointment, however, he quickly realized Sellers had other ideas.

"Troy will collapse on Nick the second we inbound the ball," the coach was saying, sketching shaky *X*s and *O*s with a marking pen on a white board on the floor at the center of their huddle. "For that reason, Nick, I want you to line up on the baseline off the key on the left side. Stewart will take the ball into The Rock, here, who will dribble toward you, but then suddenly whip a pass over to Ted, here, beside the free-throw line. Ted, you'll take the last shot."

Ted didn't know if he liked that idea. He was their best outside shooter—after Nick, of course—but he'd been having an off night, hitting four of fourteen from the field. He stared at the *X*s and *O*s as if they were part of a ticktacktoe game he had just lost. "What if they don't collapse on Nick?" he asked, standing beside The Rock. "Then I could have both their guards in my face."

"Go Nick! Set the pick! Let your best shot rip!"

"Their guards should fall back," Coach Sellers said, not sounding very sure of himself. "But if they don't, you'll have to take the ball higher up and take a longer shot."

"What if I miss?" Ted asked.

"Then we lose the game and you're the goat," The Rock said.

"That's enough of that," Coach Sellers said.

"Go Ted! Use your head! Make the Trojans drop dead!"

"I wish to God they'd shut up," Ted said. "Don't we have another play?"

"Don't you want to take the last shot?" Coach Sellers asked.

"Sure," Ted said. "I just don't want to miss it."

Coach Sellers glanced at each of them, clenching and unclenching his fingers. *"Do* we have another play?" he asked.

"Let me pass the ball down to Nick," The Rock said.

"It's too obvious a move," Coach Sellers said. "He'll have someone in front of him, someone behind him. You'd never get him the ball."

"Ted will never get the ball in the basket," The Rock said.

"Hey, I could make it," Ted said. "Maybe."

"Go Rock! Be a jock! Catch the ball and give 'em a sock!"

"Who writes those bloody things?" The Rock growled.

Nick felt he should speak up. He could line up a couple of feet closer to the basket than the coach wanted, catch the ball on the leap, and spin around and bank it in. The Rock had improved two hundred percent as a passer in the last week. It would be a sound play. The coach was looking at him. They were all looking at him, waiting. Nick glanced behind him, at the jammed bleachers. He'd seen Maria up there when he'd been warming up before the second half. And her parents. He remembered them from Alice's party.

What if I miss?

Suddenly, although he had enjoyed their support all night, he could feel the weight of the crowd. This week, for the first time since his move to this part of town, walking around campus had not been an ordeal. Rather than jumping out of his way, people had been stopping him to wish him luck. But would these same people laugh behind his back next week if he blew the team's last chance? He had already had a great game. Prudence dictated he play it safe.

"Whatever you say, coach," he mumbled finally, taking the easy way out and hating himself for it.

Coach Sellers nodded nervously, glanced at Ted. "You'll make it," he said.

Ted swallowed. "Christ."

The time-out ended. Wiping the last beads of perspiration from his hands with his towel, Nick followed his teammates back onto the court, positioning himself near the baseline, to the left of the basket. A moment later Troy's center came and stood at his back, while Troy's power forward placed himself a few feet in front, between him and Stewart. Nick knew Troy's forward would drop back and lean on him, try to box him in, the moment the referee handed Stewart the ball. Both their center and power forward—in fact their whole team—were strong, very physical.

Oh, no! We forgot to tell Ted to get off his shot early enough for me to stand a chance at a rebound.

Nick went to speak to Ted precisely when the referee tossed the ball to Stewart and blew the whistle. That settled that. Stewart now had five seconds to inbound the ball. Ted would have to follow the cheerleaders' advice and use his head.

Troy's power forward immediately jumped back and sagged into Nick. Their center put a hand on his shoulder, a hand that might have had a hold on his jersey. Nick did not struggle to get free, deciding to wait a moment to see which way—figuratively and literally—the ball bounced.

Free of defensive pressure, Stewart easily inbounded the ball to The Rock. Unfortunately, as The Rock dribbled toward Nick, only one of Troy's guards moved to block his path. The other kept his position near the top of the key, near Ted. The seven on the clock slipped to five.

Putting forth a faked shot that probably didn't fake a person in the building, The Rock whizzed the ball

177

over to Ted, who caught it a solid twenty feet from the basket. Then Ted did the strangest thing. He paused to study the ball, as if he were checking to see if it were the brand name he would willingly have chosen to use while risking his athletic reputation. He did this for a grand total of perhaps one second. Given the situation, that was an extremely long time. Never give the ball to someone who's afraid of it, Nick thought. Michael was right, Sellers should coach checkers. The clock went to three seconds.

Ted finally emerged from his important study, but with no clear idea of what he wanted to do next, whether to dribble closer or shoot. The crowd screamed, clearly wishing he would make up his mind. Ted glanced at Troy's advancing guard, decided to put the ball up. Nick knew it wasn't going to go down before it left his hands. Ted launched it toward the backboard as if he were throwing a stone at an attacking dinosaur.

Nick pivoted to his left, slapping off the hold on him with his elbow, crashing into the key, into perfect position to grab the rebound. Ted's shot didn't even hit the rim, however, and had so much behind it that it ricocheted high off the backboard. Nick not only had to leap as he had never leaped before to catch it, but he had to twist back so that his midsection stretched directly across the face of Troy's big center.

Time did not slow down for Nick as he had often heard it did in moments of crisis. Indeed, as he rolled prone off the center's nose, the ball balanced precariously in his right hand, the floor five feet beneath the back of his head and getting closer fast, he caught a glimpse of the big red letters on the clock going from two to one. He acted instinctively. He scooped the ball toward the basket, feeling a painful slap to his right arm in the process. The slap, though, didn't hurt nearly so much as his butt did when he hit the floor.

Go in! Go in!

From flat on his back on the floor, Nick watched the ball roll lazily around the inside of the rim. The crowd gasped. The buzzer sounded. The ball rolled out.

We lost.

The disappointment soaked through him like a bitter drink, draining away his energy. He couldn't even be bothered getting up. But there was The Rock, his fat hand out, insisting he do so.

"You can do it, buddy," The Rock said, clasping Nick's wrist and yanking him to his feet. "Two free throws and this baby's wrapped."

"What are you talking about? It's over."

"You were fouled, man."

The Rock's comment was slightly premature. The refs—and the coaches—were still arguing about it. Nick had never seen Coach Sellers so alive; all that blood in his cheeks.

Standing with his teammates, waiting anxiously for the decision, Nick spotted someone that almost caused him to faint.

His father was standing at the top of the bleachers.

A moment later the crowd cheered. Coach Sellers returned to his seat and began to twitch. Ted and The Rock patted Nick on the butt. The referee handed him the ball. Nick stared at it a moment.

It's a Spalding, Ted. A fine brand.

Nick had trouble locating the free-throw line. It seemed to him someone had moved it back a few feet. He had shot about sixty-five percent from the field tonight, but had taken six free throws and made only two. Standing at the line, alone on the floor—time had officially expired—he bounced the ball a couple of times and listened as the ear-busting din dropped to a heart-stopping silence. This wasn't pressure. This was murder.

Nick glanced up at his father. His father had only

remarked upon his going out for the team once; that had been to tell him it had better not interfere with his bringing home his weekly check.

Why is he here?

Nick tried to focus on his grip on the ball, the position of his feet behind the line, the basket, trying to envision the ball sailing through the air and swishing through the net. He dribbled twice more, took a deep breath, and closed his eyes. But he felt himself beginning to sway and quickly opened them. Yet the dizziness did not leave.

I am going to miss.

As it was, feeling the way he did, he would be putting up a couple of shots reminiscent of Ted's last attempt. The problem was, he couldn't jump, pivot, or fall away. Custom said he had to stand there relatively still and either make it or miss it. His decision after practice on Thursday notwithstanding, this was not his world. He was but a visitor. He had to obey custom.

He glanced again to his father. Although faraway—two hundred feet, at least—it seemed to Nick their eyes met. His dad did a little jump where he stood, pumping with his arms and nodding.

Do it your own way, but do it.

Nick turned and took a fifteen-foot jump shot.

He made it.

The crowd cheered.

He took another jump shot. *Swish*. Game over: Tabb 58, Westminister 57. The crowd freaked.

Like a wave bursting a dam, people flooded the court. Nick felt his own wave breaking inside. He felt, without a speck of worry or pain to blemish it, a clear white euphoria.

He got touched more in the next few minutes than he had been touched in his entire life; guys and girls pumping his hands, slapping him on the back, telling him how great he was. He drank it up like a man dying of thirst would have drunk down a barrel of Gatorade, which, by the way, was exactly what The Rock had decided to pour over Nick's head.

Then his dad was congratulating him, along with Mr. Gonzales. Nick introduced them, sounding to his own ears as if he were babbling in a foreign language, but making enough sense to get them shaking hands and talking basketball strategy.

And somewhere in all this, Maria appeared. Climbing to her tiptoes, she asked if she could speak to him outside. He let himself be led into the cold and the dark, down a hallway, and behind a tree. Here she didn't compliment him on his defense or his lay-ups. She had never been one to talk a lot.

"I'm sorry," she said. "Can you forgive me?"

"No problem," Nick said. In that instant, he honestly felt all his problems were behind him. He kissed her.

Jessica had taken her pictures and stowed her camera when she spotted Michael slipping away from the jubilant crowd out the corner doorway. She jumped after him, but had a few hundred people in her way, and didn't catch him until he was far down a black empty covered walkway outdoors. He didn't stop to see who was following him until she called his name.

"Hi, Jessie," he said pleasantly, turning. "Great game, wasn't it?"

"It was fantastic. But I wish you could have played."

"I'm busy enough these days. Going to change for the dance now?"

"Yeah, I have this long yellow dress I bought." She forced a laugh. "I'll probably be tripping over it all night."

"Yellow suits you. I'm sure you'll look very beautiful."

She wished she could see his face better, see if he was just being polite, or if she really was beautiful to him. She needed courage. There was so much she wanted to say. "You're coming, aren't you?" she asked.

"No, I don't think so. I'm not much of a dancer. And I have work to do."

That must mean he was leaving the campus. Yet he had not been walking toward the parking lot. Her heart was breaking. More than anything, she had wanted to dance with him. "But you can't work on a night like this. It can't be that important?"

"To me it is." He paused. "Did you call and get your SAT scores?"

"Not yet," she lied. And one lie always led to another, and suddenly she realized she didn't have the strength to confess how weak she was, or how strong she could be if he would come with her.

"Let's hope for the best," he said.

"Yeah."

He touched her arm. "It's cold out here. You'd better get inside." He smiled. "Have lots of fun for me."

She nodded sadly. "I will." Letting go of her arm, he turned and walked away. "Michael?" she called.

He stopped. "Yeah?"

I would love to love you.

"Nothing," she said, knowing as she watched him walk away that the moment had come and gone. Gone for good.

CHAPTER TWENTY

As planned, the four girls—Maria, Jessica, Sara, and Polly—met in room HB-22 to dress for the dance. A number of rooms had been unlocked for girls to change in. The game had ended at eight and Sara had already warned the student body via an announcement in homeroom that morning that no one would be allowed into the tent before nine. Parents of the girls on the court, the announcement had further stated, would be welcome to stop by at ten-thirty for the crowning. Sara's own mother had wanted to come to the dance but Sara had told her not to dare. She hadn't been getting along with her parents since Russ had moved in. They were probably worried he was having sex with her in the middle of the night. But so far, she'd had no such luck.

"How do I look?" Jessica asked, a yellow ribbon in her hair to match her yellow gown.

"Wonderful," Maria said, excited, wearing a relatively plain white dress, no ribbon.

"Great," Polly said, still in the clothes she had worn to the game and showing no signs of getting out of them.

"You look like Jessie dressed up," Sara said, thinking that it was Jessica's night, that no one was going to touch her. She glanced down at her own orange dress, which had squeezed her father's credit card for a tidy two hundred and sixteen dollars plus tax. "How about me?"

"Real pretty," Maria said.

183

"Pretty as a pumpkin pie before you put it in the oven," Jessica said.

"Shut up," Sara said.

They finished with their makeup, gave up trying to convince Polly to go home and put on something nice, and tumbled out of the room for the tent.

"Maria, Jessie," Sara said as they walked down the outside walkway, freezing to death without their sweaters, Polly struggling to keep up with her bad foot. "Check on the band and the servers for me. I want to take Polly and have a look at the float."

"What exactly are we checking with them about?" Jessica asked.

"It doesn't matter. That they're ready. Just talk to them, Jessie."

They split up when they reached the tent, Jessica and Maria disappearing inside. By this time Polly was really dragging. Sara felt a twinge of guilt that she'd swiped Russ from the McCoy mansion when Polly wasn't looking. Yet Polly appeared unconcerned about Russ's whereabouts and determined to enjoy the night.

A number of students were milling around outside the tent as Sara and Polly circled to the back. Several called out to Sara complaining about the cold and asking why she didn't let them in.

"Go wait in the gym," she said. "And quit hassling me."

The float surpassed Sara's expectations. That Tony Foulton had some imagination. Although she had given him a general idea of what she wanted—"a castle look to go with our queen and princesses"—it was very much his creation. A blue-carnation moat circled the entire float. Lying across the front was a fake drawbridge—a wide sheet of board, cleverly painted with black and gray strips to resemble whatever it was drawbridges were supposed to be made of. In the center of the drawbridge stood the microphone.

The plan was for Sara to announce the new queen after receiving the sealed envelope from Mr. Bark, who would emerge from inside the castle proper. It was a fond dream of Sara's that he would hand her the envelope and not feel compelled to make a speech.

Last year's homecoming queen had flown in special for the occasion from an Ivy League college back east. The latest word, however, had her at home sick from a crash fast she had undertaken to lose the forty pounds she needed to lose to fit into the dress she had worn when she had been elected queen. On top of everything else, Sara would now be doing the actual crowning.

The castle had four battlement towers, all at the front, interconnected by a plank that would be invisible to the audience. They were approximately five feet higher than the moat, decorated primarily with chrysanthemums, each a different color: gold, red, green, yellow. Four towers for four princesses.

At the back, inside the castle walls—another six feet higher than the battlement towers—stood the queen's throne. Whoever had her name in the envelope would ascend a hidden ladder behind the castle after the announcement and take up her rightful seat. (Sara had swiped the chair from her own living room.) With the lights flashing and the band playing, Sara thought they could do the MTV video she had stolen the concept from one better.

"This thing isn't going to fall over?" Sara asked Polly.

"It's possible," Polly said. "Anything is possible."

"Swell," Sara said. Yet she trusted Tony's skill.

Kats appeared from beneath the float. Bubba had explained to Sara that Kats bore Tabb High a measure of resentment for the way everybody had treated him while he had been in high school. Playing an essential role in the homecoming festivities, Bubba had thought, would help dispel the resentment. Sara would have preferred a driver who had a positive outlook, but she had decided to be diplomatic about the issue, hoping Bubba would forget the sex contingency he had tied to his assistance. She still didn't know what was going on with the money she had given him.

"It's dark in there," Kats said.

"Will you be able to see where you're going?" Sara asked.

Kats pointed to Polly. "Hey, Alice was your sister, right?"

Polly lowered her head. "Yes."

"I asked you a question?" Sara said, annoyed at his lack of tact.

Kats grinned. "I'll take care of you ladies, never fear."

They left Kats and slipped inside through the folds in the tent. The band was already on the stage. The food, the glasses, the plates, the silverware—everything was laid out. Ringing the entire canvas dance floor were four dozen electric heaters, glowing orange and warm. The temperature inside the tent was variable, with drafts and cold spots, but Sara believed it would even out when all the people were crammed together.

Polly collapsed into a seat near the punch. Jessica came up to Sara. "They're beginning to jam up outside," she said.

Sara glanced at her watch. "It's fifteen minutes early. Oh, what the hell, let's strike up the band and let them in."

"But you don't have anyone stationed to collect tickets."

Sara realized Jessica was right. She had forgotten

all about that. "Let them all in." She laughed. "Who cares? Let's party."

Michael had gone through nineteen files and was initiating a search on the twentieth when he began to believe he was wasting his time. So far, the name *McCoy* had not rung a bell with any of ARC's records.

He could hear the music from the dance, the laughter and jeers of people having fun. He tried to remember when he'd last had a good time through a whole night, and couldn't. He would've liked to have seen Jessica in her yellow dress.

Michael started the search on the file and got up and walked about the room, stretching. Half the overhead fluorescent lights had died moments after he returned to the computer room at the end of the game. His eyes were aching from staring at the bright green CRT letters and numbers. Earlier in the day, someone must have spilt something in the biology room next door. There was a foul smell in the air. He felt vaguely claustrophobic, as if he were being forced to labor in a morgue.

Now that it had come down to it, he almost hoped he didn't find the autopsy report. He felt as if he were trying to dig up Alice's body.

Are these the days everyone says we'll remember as the happiest days of our lives? Jessica wondered. *God.*

Bill had just brought her a drink. Jessica wished he had brought her a real drink. Something to numb the pain. Yet she really shouldn't have been drinking at all. As it was, shaking from nerves over the upcoming announcement, she was running to the bathroom in the gym every twenty minutes to pee. And her stomach was upset. She had tried to eat something, thinking it would help, but had accidentally bitten her tongue, soaking her mouthful of chicken sandwich with blood and grossing out her stomach further. Luckily, Bill had not tried to kiss her so far. She imagined she wouldn't taste very good.

"How's your drink?" Bill asked.

Jessica sipped it without enthusiasm. "Great."

They were standing with a group of football players and their girlfriends at the edge of the dance floor not far from the band. The music was excellent: present-day pop and sixties rock classics. But the volume was way too high; it was giving her a headache. Bill and she had danced once, to "Surfer Girl," slow and close. In his dark blue suit, his blond hair short and clean, he had to be the cutest guy under the tent. He'd put his arms around her and held her to his chest, where she found herself living a fantasy from the early days of the school year, but which now brought her no pleasure.

"Having a good time?" Bill asked.

Jessica smiled. "Super."

It was a night of firsts for Nick. He had never been a hero before, or a boyfriend. Now he was both, and although he couldn't say which brought him more satisfaction, he hoped he was to enjoy the two roles for a long time.

Like Maria in his arms, the music was soft as they slowly danced over the dimly lit floor. He had never danced before, either, but he had been delighted to find it a lot easier than attempting to shoot a basketball with three guys hanging on to him. The feeling of warmth where Maria's body touched his was flowing straight to his brain, sending his blood and thoughts swimming. His only concern was that she was getting a crick in her neck trying to look up at him.

"I can't believe my father went off with your parents," Nick said, his big hands resting on top of her black hair.

"He's usually not very sociable?"

"Sort of. He hates almost everybody."

Maria chuckled. "Does he speak much Spanish?"

"Some. Do your parents speak much English?"

"A little." Maria smiled up at him. "They'll be all right. They have things in common."

"Basketball?"

"Us."

"Oh." He liked the sound of that little word. It gave him confidence. Yet, remembering she was an illegal alien, he hesitated before asking his next question. "So, Maria, you no longer feel afraid to be seen by people?"

She chuckled again. "I haven't been wearing a bag over my head at school." Then she was serious. "I have Jessica to thank for tonight. She told me to bring my parents to the game. She's the one who put my name on the homecoming-court ballot."

"I feel the same way about Mike. He forced me to go out for the team." Nick laughed. "He forced me to ask you out on our date."

Maria stepped back and lightly socked him, but he grabbed her hand and pulled her closer and they went right on dancing. He rested his chin atop her head. "Are you worried about winning tonight?" he asked after a while.

She poked his chest with her nose. "I've already won."

Not long after Maria socked Nick, Russ tried to kiss Sara in the middle of a dance. Sara held her head back.

"What's wrong?" he demanded. "You kissed me the other night?"

"There're people here." She glanced to the chair on the other side of the floor where Polly had sat the whole night, Alice's sketch pad balanced on her knees, drawing. Sara had brought her some punch a half hour ago and glanced at her work, a rather poor—though elaborate—drawing of the float and the four princesses. Sara had not known what Polly was trying to say by putting a big clock about to strike twelve on the front of the queen's tower.

Does she think all the princesses are going to turn into pumpkins?

"So?" Russ said, annoyed.

"So, I'm ASB president, I can't be seen kissing a boy in front of everybody like an ordinary girl."

"If you don't kiss me right now, I'll fondle your breasts in front of everybody."

Why doesn't he get urges like this when we're alone?

"You wouldn't dare!"

"No?" He went to grab her chest with both his paws. She jumped back and scurried past him.

"Excuse me, Russ, I've got to go beat the bank."

She had spotted Bubba, alone, taking a break from tearing up the floor on every song with Clair. One thing you had to hand Clair, she didn't give a hoot—unlike Jessica—about being seen with a fashionable guy. Personally, Sara thought Jessica would have done a lot better with Michael Olson instead of Bill Skater. You could talk to Michael. From watching Bill in political science, Sara had decided he was essentially a blank sheet.

"Where's the money?" she asked, tapping Bubba on the shoulder. He turned to face her, smiling serenely, alcohol on his breath. Obviously he had brought his own private punch.

"Where's your body?" he asked.

"Why is it that all of a sudden everyone wants my body?"

"Did you sell it to someone else?"

She glared. "That isn't funny. Do you have the

money to pay for this dance or not? And don't give me any BS."

"Why the harsh tone?" Bubba gestured to the rest of the tent. "None of this would have been possible without my assistance. Look about you and be grateful."

Sara had to admit he was right; the dance was a stunning success. Three-quarters of the student body must have come, as opposed to last year's homecoming when less than three hundred tickets had been sold. The music, the food, the colorful ribbons and ornaments hanging across the tent—everything was perfect. Everybody seemed to be having a great time. Already tonight, she'd been stopped a dozen times and congratulated on what a fantastic job she'd done.

But he's still trying to screw me.

"It is I who should be disappointed with you," Bubba continued, leaning closer. "I've done all this and received nothing in return. But, I must say, you do seem in a frisky mood tonight, Sara, dear. Why don't we get together at my place after I drop—"

"Can it. You've done nothing for me. I spoke to the caterer and the band. They say we still owe them half their money."

"Then repay me fifty percent tonight. You know what really turns me on and doesn't take a lot of time? Later, in my bedroom, if you could take off your dress and—"

"Stop it! Where's the money?"

Bubba belched. "I lost it."

"You lost it!" she screamed. People—probably more than would have bothered to look had Russ actually succeeded in fondling her breasts—turned their heads. "How could you lose it?" she hissed.

He shrugged. "Money comes and goes, just like girls and bad weather. It's the way of things."

It was a frightening thing, feeling this close to wanting to murder someone. "If you lost it all, how did you pay for any of this?" she demanded.

"Oh, I had to borrow some more."

"From who?"

"Friends of the family."

She had heard rumors about his family. "Are you talking about loan sharks?"

"Shh. They don't like that word. Never use it around them. They might get angry."

She grabbed him by his bright green tie. "You don't know the meaning of the word *angry!* I am not going to pay loan-shark interest rates on a loan you had no right to take out!"

He laughed. "You sure are a spunky little girl."

She yanked on the tie, choking him. "I mean it!"

He calmly reached up and removed her hand, straightening his tie and the green hat on his fat head. "I'm afraid you have no choice, Sara. I told you at the beginning, I'm not going to bring my own personal funds into this matter. But don't despair. I borrowed enough to make the first couple of payments. And it's six months till June, a long time before you'll need big money for another big event. I'll think of something between now and then." He added slyly, "If you're nice to me, that is."

She sneered, absolutely disgusted. "I hate you."

He beamed. "Not as much as I love you, Sara."

Stalking back to Russ, she was apprehended by Mr. Bark. He wanted her to gather the princesses outside behind the float. It was time to crown the queen.

If it had been cold outside before, it was freezing now. Jessica didn't know if she could stand to wait any longer in her short sleeves with the other girls on the basketball courts. A wind had begun to blow; it kept picking at the hem of her dress, sending goose-flesh up her legs. Maria was the only smart one among them. She had on Nick's jacket, and on Maria it was as good as a full-length coat.

"Won't the truck under the float start?" Maria asked.

Sara had raved to Jessica about how neat the float was, but looking at it waiting in the dark fifty yards off the rear of the tent, its numerous towers reminding her more of an obstacle course than a castle, Jessica wished the announcement were taking place on stage in front of the band. What a joke; Sara was always calling her a snob, and here Sara had obviously put together this float solely for the purpose of being remembered as the greatest president Tabb High had ever had.

"It starts fine; it just keeps stalling," Jessica said. She could hear Kats and Sara arguing inside. It seemed Sara had rigged a hose to the exhaust tail of the truck so the fumes could be funneled away from the float. Kats wanted the hose removed. The fumes kept backing up inside the tail pipe, he said, and were choking the engine.

"Do what he says and let's get this thing over with," Clair called out, standing near the front of the float with Cindy Fosmeyer. Clair had selected blue for the color of her gown, but even if she'd chosen bright stripes and polka dots, Jessica thought, she still would have been beautiful. But Jessica was finding it difficult to understand how Cindy Fosmeyer had been selected to the court. The girl had lost several pounds in the past week—perhaps as much as half a pound directly off her massive chest—but her large nose had not shrunk in the interim and the ton of makeup she had chosen to plaster over her face had failed to bury it. It was a sad fact, but a fact nevertheless: Cindy was a dog.

After a few more encouraging remarks from Clair— each one containing a few more cuss words—Sara finally relented and did what Kats wanted. She removed the hose, but muttered that they had better hold their breath for the duration of the ride into the tent.

Mr. Bark appeared. An envelope in his right hand, he crouched down behind the queen's castle, while Sara stationed herself inside the moat up front. Clair and Cindy got onto the battle towers on the left. Jessica was the last one up, taking the tower on the far right—facing the float—off to Maria's left. Beneath them, Kats turned over the truck's engine.

"Go slow," Sara called down to Kats, who was invisible beneath their feet. Sara raised a walkie-talkie to her mouth. "We're coming," she said, telling whoever it was inside to start the music and raise the curtains.

What followed next irritated Jessica's finer sensibilities, yet at the same time gave her a big rush. In reality, she was as much a sap for flash and glitter as the next teenage girl.

The float rocked forward. In front, the tent walls began to part, slowly revealing row upon row of couples waiting within a spell of pulsing synthesized rhythms and whirling strobe lights, looking like a futuristic gang of kids partying aboard a huge spaceship.

They passed beneath the ceiling of the tent. A searchlight caught the tip of the float. The true colors of the castle flooded Jessica's eyes, dazzling her. The searchlight rolled over her face and practically blinded her. She could smell the fumes Sara had spoken of, could hear the eerie sci-fi music. But the next thing she actually saw was the float swaying—as Kats brought it to a halt—and Sara stepping up to the microphone.

Heavy stuff.

Kats shut off the truck. The canvas closed at their

back, and the temperature leaped into the comfort zone.

"Having a good time?" Sara asked to the crowd, getting an immediate earsplitting "Yeah!" "That's good, that's great," she went on. "I know it's been a while since I last spoke to all of you at once. And there's something I said that day I'd like to take back. Getting ready for this dance with the help of the whole ASB council, I've learned a high school really does need class officers. I've also discovered that you'd have to be out of your mind to want to be one." The audience laughed and Sara continued smoothly. "But let's get down to business. Let's crown our new queen. I'll start by introducing the members of the court." Sara gestured to her right. "Over here, at a hundred and ten pounds and undefeated in all her previous fights, we have blond and blue-eyed Clair Hilrey!"

Clair—much to Jessica's displeasure—accepted the silly introduction by raising both her arms high like a prizefighter, showing everyone that—besides being able to take a joke—she had the best body on the float. The audience loved it.

Her reputation sure has bounced back.

"Ooh, baby!" Bubba's voice wailed from somewhere at the rear.

"Next," Sara said. "Beloved of the entire male population of Tabb High for her forward-reaching expression and her twin mounds of feminine excellence—Cindy Fosmeyer!"

I cannot believe she said that.

Cindy didn't seem to mind the compliments, no doubt because she didn't understand them. Politely applauding, Jessica wondered what Sara would say about her. But not half so much as she wondered what name was written in the envelope Mr. Bark carried.

Sara nodded to her left. "And now we come to the

smallest girl in the group. Small in size, but big in heart. Ladies and gentlemen, Maria Gonzales!''

The applause for Maria was warm but lacked the enthusiasm the previous two girls had enjoyed; understandable, since Maria was all but unknown on campus outside a tiny circle of friends. Her election to the court made less sense than Cindy's.

The applause died down. Sara grinned wickedly. Jessica lowered her head and began to squirm, feeling sweat forming beneath the layer of deodorant she had rolled on earlier. Sara had just better remember, she swore to herself, that they were best friends.

Oh, no.

"As most of you know," Sara began, "our final princess and I have been best friends for many years. Now I know somebody out there must be asking him or herself the question: 'can we trust good old Sara to read out anybody's name but that of her best friend?' " Sara paused, then giggled. "We'll see, won't we?" She spread out her left arm. "Wish Jessica Hart lots of luck, folks!"

Her heart pounding so hard it was close to skipping, Jessica rated her applause the loudest of the lot.

I'm in. It's me. It's got to be me!

"The envelope, please," Sara said, turning to welcome Mr. Bark as he emerged from behind the queen's tower. The chatter in the audience halted. Jessica raised her head. Sara took the envelope from Mr. Bark—snatched it from him actually—and quickly began to tear it open. Before she could finish, however, Mr. Bark wedged himself between her and the microphone.

"If I may say a few words before the crowning," Mr. Bark began.

"Damn," Sara mumbled under her breath—soft enough so that no one in the crowd seemed to hear—trying to get the slip of paper out of the envelope while trying to maintain her position behind the mike. Mr. Bark gave her an uncertain glance before continuing.

"I am happy so many of you were able to make it tonight," he said, stretching his head in front of Sara's face. "Homecoming is an important event, not only as a social occasion, but as a time to reflect upon our bigger home, the world we live in. It is a beautiful world but a fragile one. At any instant, on either side of the ocean, a button could be pushed and—"

"How many here are against nuclear war?" Sara suddenly broke in, raising her hand holding the torn envelope. The whole assembly threw their fists into the air and cheered. "Wow, we're convinced!" she exclaimed. "We'll have the petition at the door, and no one leaves here tonight without signing it. A big hand for Mr. Bark, please! Thank you!"

More clapping. Mr. Bark scowled down at Sara, and she smiled up at him. He must have realized he had nowhere to go with his speech now that she had stolen his thunder. He climbed down from the float.

The silence settled again upon the audience, quicker this time, and deeper. Sara, alone behind the microphone—a beam of light bright on her orange dress—finished opening the envelope and took out the slip of paper. Jessica did not have on her glasses, naturally, and therefore did not have a clear view of Sara's face. Yet Sara was only a few feet away, and it seemed to Jessica she froze as she unfolded the tiny white paper. But only for an instant.

Jessica Hart! Way to go Jessie! Let's hear it for Jessie!

Then Sara turned toward her, catching her eye. Beyond Sara, on the other side of the float, Clair leaned forward. The crowd waited. Everybody on the float waited.

Everybody—except Jessica. Because as Sara had

looked at Jessica, Sara's lower lip trembled slightly. Jessica saw it, and knew it was the one thing Sara did to show disappointment.

I can't believe it. I lost.

Jessica lowered her head again, her hair covering her face. She didn't see Sara turn back to the microphone, although she heard her clearly enough.

"Ladies and gentlemen, please welcome Tabb High's new homecoming queen—Maria Gonzales!"

The rest was a blur for Jessica. Maria reached for her first, and Jessica hugged her. She kissed Maria, laughed and cried with her, telling herself she was happy for her. But she cried more than the occasion deserved.

Then the other princesses were congratulating Maria, and Sara was placing the crown on top of her head and wrapping the royal robe around her frail shoulders. Music played, lights flickered. The applause went on and on. Sara directed Maria toward the back of the float. Ascending the hidden ladder, a bouquet of red roses in her arms, Maria reached the top of the tower. There she stood radiant and tall.

But even the small have far to fall.

The thought flickered past the lowest edge of Jessica's conscious mind, disappearing almost before she knew she'd had it.

Maria waved her flowers, wrapped safe in the audience's adulation.

Clair leaned over and whispered to Jessica. "As long as it wasn't you, dearie."

"I feel the same way," Jessica replied.

Michael had found the file; he had reached the cemetery. The computerized search was now leading him through data that clearly made up Dr. Gin Kawati's autopsy reports. Her tombstone was close. Any second now, he knew, he would have to take up the shovel and dig. He was literally trembling with excitement, with horror. He glanced at his watch: a quarter after one. Alice had died just after one in the morning.

Michael stood and again paced the room, as he had done so many times during the course of the night. He no longer felt simply claustrophobic; he felt as if he were smothering. His eyes burned; he hated to think what he would look like in a mirror. Part of it was from exhaustion, but the stink from the biology room had continued to assault his senses all night. He had finally identified the smell—formaldehyde. But he had not gone to wipe it up. For some reason, he was afraid to leave the computer, afraid the information on the disc might suddenly vanish.

He hadn't heard anything from the direction of the tent in the last hour. No music, no laughter. He was surprised Bubba had not dropped by after the dance to check on how the search was progressing. But Michael couldn't blame him. Clair had probably invited him back to her place. Michael would have liked to have known who the new queen was. He hoped it was Jessica, although he realized that would make her even more unattainable.

He was about to return to his seat at the terminal when he became aware of an unusual sound outside. He paused, standing in the middle of the room, and listened. He thought someone must be knocking hard on a nearby door. Then he dismissed that possibility. Whoever it was would have had to have been knocking with a battering ram. The door—if that was what it was—sounded as if it were disintegrating.

Michael reached for the door to investigate further. A beep at his back stopped him. Turning, he saw the word *Found* flashing at the top of the computer screen. He jumped to his feet.

Subject: Alice McCoy. Age: 14. Coroner: Dr. Gin Kawati.

Forgetting all about the sound, Michael began to read.

The dance was history. The cleanup had begun.

Jessica and Sara had changed from their gowns back into the clothes they had worn to the basketball game. Along with Maria, they were trying to undo in a couple of hours what had taken weeks to put together. It was a hopeless task. If the amount of fun had by all was proportional to the amount of mess they had made, then Sara's place in Tabb's history as the best ASB president was already secure.

Polly had hung around at first and tried to lend a hand, but watching her hop pathetically about with plates and glasses balanced in her arms, Jessica and Sara had sent her home. Maria was almost as useless. She had *not* changed out of her dress. She continued to float about beneath the deserted tent as if the crowds were still cheering her to the top of the float, a stoned smile on her lips.

All right, I'm envious. That doesn't mean I'll hate Maria from now on.

Jessica couldn't figure out how the girl had won.

"I'm tired," she complained, stuffing red ribbon in a green plastic trash bag and wiping the sweat from her eyes.

"You can't quit," Sara said, standing on a ladder above her. "This tent has to be ready to take down by tomorrow at noon or I'll have to pay for another day's rental."

"Let them take it down the way it is," Jessica said.

"Sure, right, and leave this pile of garbage out in the open where everybody can see it."

"Ask me if I care, Sara." Jessica threw down her bag. "I've had enough. I'm going to my locker, getting my books, and I'm not coming back."

"Some friend you are." Then Sara stopped, surveying the tons of junk. "Well, I guess you're right. There is too much to do. Go home and rest." She lowered her voice, nodded to the other side of the tent where Maria was gathering the carnations from the tables, smelling each one as if it were a gift from a boyfriend. "But on your way out, ask our little brown butterfly to give me a hand with the last of these ribbons."

"Will do."

Sara stared at her a moment. "You know, Jessie, you looked awful pretty tonight. It should have been you."

Jessica smiled, touched. "Wasn't in the cards, I guess."

Maria hugged Jessica when she told her she was leaving.

"I owe all this to you," Maria said, holding her tight.

"You did it yourself," Jessica said, embarrassed by the twinge of jealousy that was still there.

Maria let go, shook her head. "I lived in a box until you came along. I never went out. I never talked to boys. If it wasn't for you, I wouldn't even know Nick."

Jessica squeezed her arm. "We all get what we deserve, Maria. I really believe that."

Except for Alice, our sweet Alice.

Jessica grabbed her coat and left.

The wind had died. The cold had deepened. She had to get her homework from her locker before she could go home. Outside the tent, striding across the empty basketball courts toward the silent black buildings, Jessica looked up at the clear sky punctured with stars. Thoughts of Alice had come and now they would not leave. Jessica decided not to fight them. Sometimes when she was sad, she would remember everything in her life that had ever brought her unhappiness, and then whatever was depressing her at the moment would appear less significant, and she would feel better.

She spotted the red star she had been wondering about the night she had gone out with Bill. Again, she wished she had Michael by her side to tell her its name.

Strange how she could not remember Alice without thinking of Michael. He was always there, deep in her mind, standing beside Alice, as he had been in the painting her lost friend had been working on before she died.

I'll have to find that picture and hang it above my bed.

Lowering her gaze, Jessica quickened her pace. Soon she was under the exterior-covered walkway, her sneakers squeaking on the smooth concrete, cursing again the fact that Tabb was too cheap to keep a few lights burning throughout the night. With the roof from the class wing above her head and the branches of some of Tabb's oldest trees off to her side, she was in a dark place, so dark she could barely see her hand in front of her face.

As a child, the dark had both fascinated and frightened her. During the day, when the sun was bright, she had loved nothing better than to go exploring with Polly in a big sewer that was the sole source and inspiration for a creek that ran through a jungle of a lot not far from their houses. The lot was later to become a park, and then the site of another housing tract, but in those days, it had been *the* big outdoors. They must have been five or six at the time. The last time Jessica could remember exploring the tunnel with Polly—their legs spread wide so they wouldn't step in the smelly water that ran down the center, their heads bent low, flashlights swiped from Polly's garage gripped tight in each of their tiny grubby grips—had been the time they had brought Alice with them. *That* had been a mistake.

They were farther into the tunnel than they had ever been before. They had been walking forever. They were excited. Of course it was a big dream of theirs to get to the other end of the thing. They had this idea that if they could get that far, then the dimensions of the world—or at least of their neighborhood—would make more sense. Then they would know where they stood in the scheme of things.

They could see no light up ahead. But a noise had begun to throb around them, a slow thumping sound that reminded Jessica of a giant heart—not the heart of a person, but the heart of a huge machine, a machine that she imagined made all the cars and buildings and sewers. When they got to that noise, she thought, they would really know what was happening.

She never did find out what the noise was.

Alice slipped, smack into the slime in the center of the sewer. Turning to rescue her, Polly dropped her flashlight and broke it. And naturally, in the heat of the moment, Jessica imagined that her flashlight was beginning to fail too. She told the others it was, and the thought of what it would be like to be trapped in the sewer without any light was enough to send them racing back at warp speed.

Oddly enough, however, once they were out, Alice had begged them to try again to reach the other end. But Alice's stinking clothes alerted their parents to what they had been doing. Their subterranean exploration days were over.

The heart of a machine.

Jessica stopped in midstride in the black walkway.

There was a noise coming from up ahead. Not the noise she had heard in the tunnel a dozen years ago. That had been deep and rhythmic. This one sounded like someone chopping wood. Yet as she listened more closely in the dark, holding her breath, her heart pounding steadily harder and harder, the gap between the chops seemed to shorten, to almost disappear altogether, to blur with her heartbeat, until they were practically a single sound, until she was feeling smaller and smaller, and standing, not in a school outdoor walkway, but far beneath the ground, with a machine over her head that made *everything*—maybe even little girls.

The sound stopped. Silence. Her heart could have stopped.

Then Jessica heard the crash. Glass, metal, and wood exploding.

Help!

She turned and ran back the way she had come. But this was not a tunnel, with only two ways to go. Suddenly it was a maze, and she didn't even have a failing flashlight to show her the way. She went right, she went left. She didn't know which way she was going. It was insane; she spent five hours, five days a week at this school. And now she was lost!

Then she froze, holding on to the corner of an exterior wall, on to the tunnel wall. When she was a child, this had never happened to her. Although as a child, she had, like every other child in the world, dreamed it a million times.

Footsteps. Rapidly approaching footsteps.

Someone was chasing her!

Jessica let out a soft moan, remembering how when the three of them had escaped from the sewer into the wonderful sunlight, they'd discovered Alice had skinned her head. How the blood had trickled from the side of Alice's head through her bright blond hair.

And how the blood had *flowed* out the back of Alice's head as she lay dead on her back on the hard floor in her parents' bedroom.

And Michael said she'd been murdered.

Jessica bolted away from the footsteps, around the corner, back down a walkway she had the terrible feeling she had run up a moment ago.

God help me. God save me.

Apparently God only helped those who helped themselves. Or those who had a better sense of direction.

She ran smack into her pursuer.

He grabbed her. She screamed.

Michael was confused, and all because of a paragraph Dr. Kawati had added to the end of the autopsy report. The other ninety-five percent of the information had been much as he had expected.

The coroner had detailed how a twenty-two-caliber bullet had entered through the roof of Alice's mouth, torn through her cerebral cortex, ricocheted off the top of her skull, and finally exited via the base of the skull. In his notes, the doctor referred several times to a sketch he had drawn tracing the path of the bullet, and to X rays he had apparently taken during the examination—neither of which was available in the data Bubba had swiped. But the absence of the sketch and the X rays was not what had Michael stumped. Nor was the analysis of her blood out of line. Alice had had no unusual chemicals in her system at the time of her death, not even alcohol. There had also been no sign that she had undergone a struggle immediately prior to her death: no flesh under her fingernails, which might have been scraped from an assailant; no scratches on her face or arms; and, at first glance, no bruises anywhere on her body.

In conclusion, the doctor had stated that the cause of death was a severe cerebral hemorrhage brought about by a self-inflicted gunshot wound.

Then he had added a note at the end.

Because the bullet traveled a complex path before exiting the head, the girl's brain was left in extremely poor shape. It is, therefore, difficult to know if the hemorrhage found in the region of the hypothalmus and thalmus was brought about by the course of the bullet or by the force of the blow to her nasal cartilage. The cartilage has a significant fracture across its entire width, which could not have been a result of the bullet's trajectory. It is the opinion of this coroner that Alice McCoy must have fractured her nasal cartilage upon hitting the floor with her face after shooting herself. As she was found lying on her back, I must assume that someone rolled her over before the police arrived. It is suggested to the investigating officers they pay special attention to this point when questioning all those involved.

A fractured nasal cartilage? That was a fancy way of saying Alice had a broken nose in addition to a hole in her head. Michael was angry—but not the least surprised—that Lieutenant Keller had withheld this information. But Michael did remember the detective repeatedly asking if anyone moved Alice after they had found her. The lieutenant had obviously been anxious to clear up the discrepancy; and yet he had closed the case without doing so.

There were two possibilities. Either someone had moved Alice's body before they reached the room, or else something other than the fall had broken her nose.

Did someone break it for her?

The bullet had clearly snaked around inside her skull before exiting at the base; nevertheless, the bullet hole in the wall had been at best only three feet off the floor. And straight into the plaster. The chances remained that Alice had been sitting when she was shot.

And if that were true, it would be almost impossible for her to have broken her nose in a fall.

Did someone hit her, hit her hard, in the face?

The coroner had also referred to an area of hemorrhage that was possibly unconnected to that caused by the bullet. That raised another question, one that was in many ways far more confusing than the others.

What?

Something large and loud crashed outside.

Michael leaped to his feet. He was out the door before he could finish asking himself the hard question.

The dark caught him off guard. For a moment he couldn't see far enough to know in which direction to run. He paused, straining to listen. It was then he heard the footsteps, racing along the hallway on the other side of the wing that housed the computer lab. He assumed the footsteps belonged to the person who had caused the crash. He set off after him.

Whoever this individual was, he couldn't make up his mind which way he was headed. He was fast, though. Michael chased him up one hallway, down another, without catching so much as a glimpse of him. But the idiot was going in circles. Michael finally decided on a different approach. He stopped and silently jogged the *other* way, away from the guy. The strategy proved effective. A minute later he ran right into him.

"Hold on there, buddy," he shouted, grabbing him by the wrists. The fellow—he wasn't that tall—struggled furiously.

"Let me go! Help!"

Michael let her go in a hurry. "Jessie?"

"Oh, thank God," she whispered, collapsing against his chest, sobbing. "Someone's chasing me, Michael."

"*I* was chasing you." He held her in his arms. He

207

never would have believed a person could shake so much and still remain earthbound. He could hardly see her face, but he could feel her hot panting breath on his neck. He brushed her sweaty hair from her eyes, hugged her tight. "Shh, you're OK. You're safe. No one's going to hurt you."

"There was this strange sound," she said, weeping. "It was like in the tunnel, and then it just blew up, and I started running, and I—I don't know." She pulled back, wiped at her eyes, dazed. "What was it, Michael?"

"Let's go see. I think the crash came from the courtyard."

Jessica grabbed his hand. "Do you think it's all right?"

He spoke calmly, although inside he was not exactly coasting along himself. "We'll be fine." He didn't want to leave her alone, even back in the computer room.

They found the varsity tree—it was lying across the snack bar. The trunk had caved in one entire wall of the building. Branches poked out dozens of glass windows. It was quite simple; someone had chopped it down. They discovered the ax resting in the grass on top of a pile of wood chips scattered beside the splintered stump. Jessica knelt to touch it. Michael stopped her.

"There could be fingerprints," he warned. He glanced about, but didn't see anybody. "Why are you here by yourself this late?"

"I was helping Sara and Maria clean up the mess from the dance. Then I was going to my locker to get my homework. Michael, why would anyone want to kill this tree?"

"I don't know. Are Sara and Maria still at the tent?"

"Yes. I think so."

The tree had not fallen in a random fashion. The

angle had been purposely chosen to cause the most destruction possible. Only a crazy person could have been behind this. In the wake of reading the conflicting details surrounding Alice's death, the thought sent a shiver through Michael. "Let's get the girls and get out of here," he said.

Before they left the scene of the crime, however, Michael changed his mind about the ax. Getting a handkerchief from Jessica, he grabbed it by the blade and took it with them.

Sara yawned. She was as beat as Jessica had complained about being. The day had gone on forever. But she was sort of sad it was all over. Russ had been disqualified in his race, Jessica had not been crowned queen, and yet many good things had happened. Ten years from now, she imagined, if she was still alive and the world was still here, she would have fond memories of homecoming.

"Maria, I'm stacking these trash bags together and then I'm out of here," Sara called.

Maria was wandering about on the float, her royal flowers in her hands. Sara had to chuckle. There was someone who was definitely unhappy to see the evening end. No doubt Maria would find it hard to fall asleep, remembering what it had been like to hear her name called out, how it had felt to ascend to the top of the queen's tower with the whole school cheering her on.

"OK," Maria said, disappearing into the back of the float.

She's doing it all over! But can I blame her?

Thoroughly amused, Sara watched as Maria slowly wound her way up the tower steps. Once at the top, Maria set down her flowers and picked up her crown, holding it high above her head in both her hands.

"We should do this every week!" Maria called.

"Somehow, I don't think it would be the same," Sara said, glancing down, twisting the tie on the trash bag in her hands. As a result—with her attention divided—she had only a vague idea of what happened next.

Out the corner of her eye, Sara received the impression that Maria had placed the crown on her head and did a little skip into the air. That was it. Then Maria appeared to dematerialize. The illusion persisted for a fraction of a second. Until Sara heard the scream and the crash, and knew the top level of the float had caved in and taken Maria with it.

She can't be dead. Please, God.

Sara scarcely remembered crossing the tent and leaping onto the float. The next thing she knew, she was staring down into a deep, mangled hole. There was sufficient light to see the worst. Maria lay sprawled over the truck's shattered windshield, her body bent at a grotesque angle. There was blood on the glass and glass in her face. She was not moving.

"I'm coming, Maria," Sara said. "I'm coming."

It was well that Michael and Jessica showed up at that moment and that Michael had an ax in his hands. Sara had no idea how to help Maria without doing more damage. Shouting for Sara to get down, Michael peeped through a crack in the tower wall, and then began to hack away with the blade. Apparently he did not feel it would be wise to attempt to free Maria by coming in from beneath the float. Sara trusted his judgment. Hanging on to Jessica in the middle of the drawbridge, Sara felt more helpless than she had ever felt in her entire life.

Michael was through the wall in a couple of minutes. Pulling away the cracked boards, he stepped down on top of the hood of the truck. Jessica and Sara crouched beside his chopped opening.

"Is she alive?" Jessica whispered, staring in horror.

There was not a great deal of blood. It was the way Maria was lying—her torso twisted like a Gumby; her chest and face pressed into the roof; her legs jammed into the steering wheel—that filled her with dread.

"She's breathing," Michael said, taking her pale wrist in his hands and feeling for a pulse. "She's alive."

"Let's get her out!" Jessica exclaimed.

"No," Michael said firmly. "We can't move her. She could have a spinal injury." He pointed to Jessica. "There's a phone at the entrance of the gym. Dial nine-one-one. Describe the situation and our location." He nodded. "Hurry."

With Jessica gone, Sara carefully stepped onto the hood beside Michael. "It's just like the party," she said bitterly.

He sighed. "It doesn't surprise me."

Pulling her Mercedes onto her street, Polly spotted Clark swinging a leg over his motorcycle parked at the foot of her driveway. Before she could reach the house, however, he had gunned the engine and roared off in the opposite direction. For a moment she contemplated going after him. But even if she had been in a Ferrari, she knew she would never have caught him. He was like a witch on a broom.

Heading up her driveway, she noticed that the front door was wide open. The house was black, and she never left for the evening without turning on at least a couple of lamps.

"Aunty," she whispered to herself, leaping out of her car.

Inside, she couldn't get a light to go on. Either Clark had fiddled with the circuit breakers or else he had broken every bulb in the house. She stumbled into the kitchen, found a candle in a drawer, and lit it on the pilot light of the stove. Creeping down the hall toward her aunt's bedroom, shadows following her along both walls, she started to cry.

Her aunt was lying on her back and staring at the ceiling. Staring without blinking. Polly set the candle down on the nearby bed stand and sat on the bed. Aunty's pupils had clouded over, like cheap marbles that had been left too long in the bright sun. Polly couldn't even tell what color her eyes had been, and this disturbed her a great deal, that she couldn't remember.

Polly picked up the old lady's mottled hand. It was soft, softer than it had been in life, and it was still warm. She had not been dead long.

She was alive when Clark was here.

Polly glanced at the ceiling and didn't see the blood dripping down that he had spoken of; nevertheless, she felt herself smothering, a black panic rising.

She fainted on top of the dead woman.

EPILOGUE

Jessica drifted in and out of reality trying to sleep on the hard brown vinyl couch in the deserted hospital waiting room. When she was awake, she watched Michael and Nick sitting in the hallway outside the room. Sometimes they would be talking quietly to each other. Other times Nick's head would be slumped back on the wall and he would be snoring softly. But always Michael would be sitting upright, and always he looked as if he were thinking. Not once, however, did she catch him looking her way. And this simple fact filled her with a sadness that went beyond reason. It made her anguish about Maria almost unbearable. There was only pain in waking.

In being alive.

Then there were her dreams. They were mostly dark thundering things without shape or reason. But there was one that had sent a knife through her heart when she had awakened from it; for it had been beautiful and filled with a joyfulness that made her chest ache to recall it.

She was in the tunnel of her childhood. Only now Michael was with her, and they were both fully grown. Alice was there also, and another blond-haired girl Jessica did not recognize. But the two girls were younger, only three or four years old. Together, with Michael leading the way with the aid of an old-fashioned lantern, they were approaching what they knew to be the end of the tunnel.

A warm yellow light began to stream over them from

213

up ahead, making their eyes shine and their hearts quicken. Then the walls of the tunnel started to dissolve, until they could see through them. Suddenly Michael smiled and extinguished the lantern. And they were standing on a sloping desert plain, with a sparkling clear sky overhead and a breeze, sweet with the fragrance of honey, wafting through their hair. In the distance were a cool green ocean and people, old friends of theirs they could hardly wait to meet again.

Behind them, Jessica caught the faint roar of a churning river and realized that the now-invisible tunnel had been a bridge over the icy water. It was, however, only a passing thought, of something that had once concerned her but which she now understood to be of no importance. Michael took her hand—Alice and her friend were dancing ahead of them—and they walked toward the place by the ocean where the day was only beginning.

She felt as if she had just been born.

A bright spot in a dreary night. Fits of reality and nightmares chased her from then on. Until she felt a hand on her arm, shaking her gently.

"Jessie, wake up. Time to get up."

Jessica opened her eyes and discovered Sara sitting beside her on the couch. Sara had begun the vigil with Jessica outside the operating room at two in the morning, but had rushed home after receiving an emergency call from her mother. It hadn't been clear exactly what the problem was.

"What time is it?" She yawned, pushing herself up with an effort, her neck stiff as a board.

"Eight-thirty," a voice said at her back. It was Michael, standing in the hazy sunlight of the waiting-room window. "The doctors say Maria's operation went well. Her parents are with her now."

"But is she going to be all right?" Jessica asked anxiously. "What did they operate on?"

214

"Her back," Michael said, coming over and sitting on the chair beside them. "It was broken."

"Is she—paralyzed?" Jessica asked.

Michael shook his head, tired. "I don't know. I don't think the doctors like to use that word. One of us might be allowed in to see her in a few minutes. Nick's gone to talk to the surgeon who performed the operation."

"At least she's alive," Sara said.

"Yeah," Michael said. "She was lucky."

"What did your mom want?" Jessica asked Sara. Her old friend grimaced.

"Bad news. The police identified the ax you guys found as the ax taken from the store where Russ used to work. They found his fingerprints on the handle. They've arrested him!"

"You can't be serious?" Jessica said.

"Can't your parents verify where Russ was at one o'clock in the morning?" Michael asked.

"No," Sara said. "He didn't go straight home after the dance."

"Where did he go?" Jessica asked.

Sara hesitated. "He says he went to a bar. But the idiot—he can't remember which one."

"That's bad," Michael said.

"You don't think he chopped down the tree, do you?" Jessica asked.

"Of course he didn't!" Sara snapped. "But while questioning him, the police learned that he'd stayed at Polly's house for a few days. They called her, and she said that she'd had the ax in the trunk of her car until last week, when it disappeared."

"What was Polly doing with the ax?" Jessica asked.

"She says she took it from Russ one night when he was drunk and trying to chop down the varsity tree."

"They believed her?" Jessica asked, amazed.

"Russ agreed with her! Except he says *I* was the

one who stopped him back then and took his ax. He's incriminated himself left and right. They're going to lock him up, I swear it.''

"No way," Jessica said.

"They might," Michael said. "When that tree fell, it caused a lot of damage."

"He should have kept his mouth shut," Sara said. "Polly should have kept her mouth shut." She sighed, rubbing her head. "I guess we can't blame her, though. Her night was as lousy as Maria's. Her aunt passed away."

Jessica groaned. "It never stops."

Sara nodded. "And to top it off, an old-time employee of her parents' company died yesterday from a work-related accident. She's got two more funerals to go to. I hope they won't be plugging her into the socket again." Sara stood. "I have to get back to the police station. I'm trying to get Russ out on bail."

"Will your parents lend you the money?" Jessica asked.

"No," Sara said. "They're being total jerks about the whole thing." She patted Jessica on the shoulder. "I'll be back later to check on Maria. I guess we should be glad things can't get any worse. See you, Mike."

When Sara was gone, Michael sat beside her on the couch. "Can I get you anything from the snack bar?" he asked.

"Thanks, I'm not hungry. Have you been up all night?"

"Yeah."

"And you don't think it was an accident?"

Her question surprised him. "It's hard to tell from what's left of the tower. Clearing a path to Maria, I messed up the evidence something awful. We may never know if someone tampered with the float."

"But you think someone did, don't you?"

He shrugged. "I'm not sure of anything these days." He glanced at her. He needed a shave. She needed a hug. "What did Sara mean when she made that remark about plugging Polly into the socket again?"

"When we were twelve, Polly's parents died. Alice must have told you. They drove off a road in the desert and their car burst into flames. Polly was with them, but was thrown free. She didn't get so much as a scratch. But she suffered from severe depression afterward, and was in the hospital for a long time. The doctors treated her with electroshock."

"What!" Michael exclaimed. "They used electroshock on a twelve-year-old girl?"

"Is that unusual?" she asked uneasily. "She had the best doctors money could buy. It seemed to help."

Michael shook his head angrily. "Electroshock has got to be the greatest evil modern psychiatry ever spawned. It alleviates people's depression by causing irreversible brain damage. The patient is no longer unhappy because he can hardly remember what was making him unhappy."

"Then why do they use it?"

"You said it: 'the best doctors money could buy.' It costs the hospital a few cents in electricity, produces superficial improvement, and makes M.D.s tons of cash." He nodded to himself. " 'The man with the electricity.' Makes sense."

"What?"

"Just something Polly said to me when I was at her house."

"Why did you go to her house?"

He realized he'd made a slip. "You know why."

"I suppose I do." She touched his arm. "Michael, you've got to let it go."

He looked away. "I can't."

"But it's tearing you apart."

"Not like it tore Maria apart," he muttered.

"What?"

"Nothing." He rested his head in his hands, his eyes on the floor. He was thinking again. "She was outside when the gun went off. We're sure of that, aren't we?"

"Who?"

"Polly. The night of the party."

"Yes, she was outside, *alone* in the backyard. And Alice was upstairs, *alone* in her parents' bedroom. Polly didn't kill her. She loved Alice."

Michael sat up. "But a crazy person could love someone and still kill her. She wouldn't need a reason why."

"You think Polly's crazy?"

"I think she's close enough not to make much difference."

"You're wrong. She may be a bit off, but she gets by. I've known her a lot longer than you."

He softened his tone. "I appreciate that, Jessie— that she's your friend. And I realize you knew her before they attached electrodes to her brain. But tell me honestly, was it the same Polly who came out of the hospital that went in?"

"Of course she wasn't the same," she said, wondering if she wasn't trying to convince herself. "She was a young girl, and she'd lost both her parents."

"I wonder if that's all there was to it."

"But you saw Polly go out to the backyard, same as me," she said, her voice growing constricted with emotion. "And you saw her come running inside when the gun went off. Believe me, I know that house. There's no way up to the master bedroom except the stairs we took. There're no trapdoors, no hidden stairways. It's physically impossible that she shot Alice. It's impossible anyone did."

Michael looked unconvinced; nevertheless, he nodded. "I can't argue with what you say. I'm sorry I brought it up. I didn't mean to upset you."

He was still feeling guilty, she knew, about the time he had yelled at her in Alice's studio after the funeral. She smiled, squeezed his arm. "You never have to apologize to me, Michael."

He blushed, or frowned, or both. "Yeah?"

"It's true. And I'll tell you why it's true."

Because you're the only one I know who's striving for perfection. Who's completely noble and totally unselfish. The only one who's always there when I need rescuing from myself.

The words did not come out, not right away, and not so much because she was embarrassed to say them, but because she was ashamed that she had stood him up on their date, that she had purposely started the rumor of Clair's abortion and accepted his help on the SAT. That she was unworthy of him.

"Jessie?" he said, waiting for her.

I can still tell him, and let him decide. About me. Us.

"Because, Michael Olson, old locker buddy—"

"Jessie," Nick called, striding into the waiting room, a different person from the guy who had led Tabb to victory the night before. He had huge bags under his eyes. He stuttered when he spoke. "The d-doctor said you can see M-Maria for a couple of minutes."

"Have you seen her?" Jessica asked, jumping up with Michael.

"She wants to see you first," Nick said, tense.

"But how is she?" Jessica asked. "Will she be able to walk again?"

"I don't know," Nick complained. "Nobody will tell me nothing. And her parents have left already."

Jessica followed Nick's directions and ended up in an aggressively green intensive-care ward. The medicine smell made her empty stomach uneasy. The patients' rooms were tiny glass cubicles arranged around a nurses' station packed with enough electronic equipment to pilot a Trident submarine. The RN on duty pointed out Maria's box and reminded her that her visit was not to exceed three minutes.

A white sheet loosely covered Maria's body; it wasn't much whiter than the color of her skin. Quietly closing the door, Jessica noted through an opening in the sheet that a plastic and metal brace was locked over Maria's bare hips. It reached all the way up her side, embracing her slim shoulders. It could not have looked more uncomfortable. Maria had her eyes open—one eye, rather; the other was swollen shut—and was staring at the ceiling.

Where else can she look?

"It's me," Jessica said.

Maria cleared her throat. "I know."

Jessica moved closer to the bed. Bandage covered the right side of Maria's face; out the bottom of it peeked a stitched cut. She would be scarred as well.

But did she sever her spinal cord?

Jessica walked over to take Maria's hand and bumped into her IV. Wires led from beneath the sheet to monitors overhead. She had to fight to keep her voice calm. "How are you, Maria?"

Her single black eye turned toward Jessica. "How do I look?"

She forced a smile. "A little under the weather. But you'll be better soon. This is a great hospital."

"Is it?"

"Oh, yeah. I had my appendix out here when I was thirteen years old. They have the best doctors. Wonderful nurses."

Maria closed her eye. "Since you love it here so much, it's too bad it wasn't you who broke her back."

"Huh?" Jessica had to force air into her lungs in order to speak. "You don't mean that."

Maria smiled, and with her cuts and swollen face, it was truly gruesome. "I remember when you talked me into putting my name on the ballot for the homecoming court. You told me this was America, that anything could happen, that I might even be nominated queen. But you didn't believe it. Had you thought I stood a chance in a million, you wouldn't have let me get within a mile of that ballot."

"You've been through a terrible ordeal," Jessica said, struggling to keep her composure. "You need to rest, to heal. And you're going to heal, Maria."

Maria looked at her again, her one eye a single accusing finger. "It should have been you standing at the top of that float. You wanted to be homecoming queen more than anything. You schemed to go out with the popular boys so you'd be popular. You told lies about Clair. You told me lies."

"Stop it. You don't know what you're saying."

"It should be you lying here instead of me!"

The tears burst from Jessica then and she had to turn away. She went to the huge window by the door. Hanging from a white thread close to the glass was a silver angel—a Christmas decoration. With everything else going on, she had forgotten that Christmas was only a couple of weeks away. She had gotten so caught up in the fantasy of being the most desired girl on campus that she had almost overlooked what had always been for her the most precious time of the year, and the realization made her feel there must be some justice in what Maria said.

I'm no longer a little girl. I've grown up. I'm a bitch.

Searching for a handkerchief in her pocket to wipe away her tears, her fingers ran into a bobby pin. An idea occurred to her. Pulling out the pin, her back to

221

Maria, she scraped off the rubbery black stuff at the ends. Then she stepped to the foot of the bed.

"They'll only let me stay a minute longer," she said, carefully lifting the sheet from Maria's toes. Maria, her eyes again closed, didn't seem to notice.

"A pity."

"I'm still your friend, no matter what you may think right now. I'll be back tomorrow to visit." Holding the pin between her thumb and index finger, she poked it gently into Maria's heel.

She should have jumped. If she could feel . . .

"Don't put yourself out."

She poked Maria harder, again and again. But the girl just lay there. She was paralyzed. Jessica began to back away from the bed, trembling. She *had* lied to her. Maria was never going to heal. Never.

"It's no trouble," she said, her voice choking. "If I can bring you anything, anything at all?"

"There is one thing I would like."

"What?"

"A promise." Maria opened her eye, but Jessica did not believe she could actually see her this close to the door.

"Yes?"

"Promise me I will never have to see you again."

Jessica swallowed hard, tasting her friend's bitterness, her own worthlessness. "Good-bye, Maria. I hope you feel better soon."

Michael was waiting with Nick by the coffee machine in the hall next to the waiting room when Jessica reappeared. Ordinarily Michael did not drink coffee; it gave him heartburn. But since he had been staying awake all night worrying whether a girl was going to lose her life or not, he had considered it sort of absurd to be concerned about minor gastric upset. This was his eighth cup since three o'clock in the morning. Nick had just downed his tenth.

Jessica was crying. Nick grabbed her as she tried to pass them by without stopping. "What's wrong with Maria?" he demanded. "Did she die?"

Jessica stared at him, her eyes big and red. She shook her head weakly. "She wants to see you now."

Nick let go of her and dashed down the hall. Jessica took a couple of feeble steps forward and then sagged against the wall. Michael put down his coffee and placed his palms on her back, over her soft brown hair, feeling her shiver. "Tell me, Jessie?"

"The fall cut her spinal cord."

"You're sure?"

"Yes."

He had feared as much. "That's very sad. But it's not the end of the world for her. She can live a full life. But she's going to need a lot of support. I know you have a lot to give her."

Jessica stood upright, looked at him, her face a mess with tears. "She hates me."

"What? No."

"She told me she wishes it was me who was crippled instead of her."

"She didn't mean it. She's just upset. Tomorrow—"

"There won't be any tomorrow!" Jessica cried. "I told you, she hates me! She doesn't want to see me again. She blames me for what happened to her."

"She came out of surgery two hours ago. You can't take what she says seriously. You didn't do anything to her. You're her friend."

"Like I'm your friend, Michael?" She shook loose from his hands. "You don't know who I am. I screw you left and right and you think I'm Miss Pretty Perfect. Well, I'm not. I don't give a damn about anybody except myself."

"We all watch out for ourselves. We have to because most of the time it seems no one is watching out for us. I know how you feel. You're not a bad person." He took a breath. "If you were, I wouldn't care about you the way—"

"No!" she interrupted. "It's all true. Everything I touch gets ruined. Alice and Maria and Clair—I do it on purpose I think!"

"Stop it. You're carrying on exactly like I did after the funeral." He lowered his voice, tried to hold her. "Jessie, listen to me, I need to tell you something."

"No," she moaned, pushing him away. "Don't touch me. Don't get near me. I'm no good, Michael. I'm not."

"Jessie?"

She wouldn't listen. She turned and fled down the hall. He didn't go after her. Had people chased after him during the days following Alice's party, he might have killed them. He would leave her alone, maybe forever. He would remain alone.

Nick returned a few minutes later. He was pale as a ghost. "Does she hate you, too?" Michael asked wearily.

Nick fell down in a chair. "She wants the person who tampered with the float," he said. "She's flipped out. She thinks there's a plot against her."

"Anything else?"

Nick nodded heavily. "She told me to find those responsible. She threatened me if I didn't."

"How?"

Nick bowed his head. "She said if I didn't do what she wanted, she would tell the police I was running down the stairs, away from the bedroom, right after the gun was fired at the party."

"That's true?"

"Yeah," he croaked. "I lied to you before. I was

224

afraid the police would hear that and think I'd killed Alice.''

It was Michael's turn to use the wall for support. ''Why were you running downstairs?''

''I thought the gunshot came from there.'' He shook his head miserably. ''I don't know, I was scared. I'm sorry, Mike.''

Kats also thought the shot came from downstairs.

Michael pulled himself off the wall and slapped Nick on the back. ''Stay with her, buddy. Love her. It's the best anybody can do. I'm going home.''

Nick nodded pitifully, beginning to weep. ''She can't feel anything in her legs. Nothing from the waist down.''

''I know. I wish—'' He wished a thousand wishes, but it didn't make any difference. There was nothing he could say. He left Nick and headed for the parking lot, where he climbed into his car. About to start the engine, he noticed Temple High's yearbook on the passenger seat. On impulse, he reached over and began to browse through it again. He hadn't really searched the book thoroughly the first time. Perhaps . . .

It could have been coincidence, like Kats and Nick both running the wrong way toward a gunshot they were closer to than anyone else.

Michael found Clark in a group photo on the lower-right-hand corner of the first page he turned to. It was a black-and-white, and the bright green eyes and red hair were not in evidence. But it was the bastard; there was no mistaking that twisted grin.

The picture had several people in it. None of them were identified at the bottom by name. Michael flipped to the end of the junior class and studied the list of names of kids who hadn't posed for pictures. There was only one Clark.

Clark Halley.

We're going to have a talk, guy. A long talk.

TO BE CONTINUED . . .

Final Friends 3:
The Graduation

The truth is finally revealed.
At a terrible price . . .

About the Author

CHRISTOPHER PIKE was born in Brooklyn, New York, but grew up in Los Angeles, where he lives to this day. Prior to becoming a writer, he worked in a factory, painted houses, and programmed computers. His hobbies include astronomy, meditating, running, playing with his nieces and nephews, and making sure his books are prominently displayed in local bookstores. He is the author of *Last Act*, *Spellbound*, *Gimme a Kiss*, *Remember Me*, *Scavenger Hunt*, *Final Friends* 1, 2, and 3, and *Fall into Darkness*, all available from Pocket Books. *Slumber Party*, *Weekend*, *Chain Letter*, *The Tachyon Web*, and *Sati*—an adult novel about a very unusual lady—are also by Mr. Pike.